she admitted. "I'm afraid I won't ever know what happened in my past. I'm afraid that I will, and won't be able to stand that knowledge. Who am I, Richard?" she asked desperately.

Slowly, almost as though he had to do so, he brought her against the strength of him. And, as though this, too, he had to do, he lowered his mouth to hers.

*She knew this touch!* Somehow, from countless longings and memories still hidden from her mind, she knew it. She sighed and surrendered to the sense of homecoming that washed over her.

But too soon she felt him drawing away from her.

"We can't do this," he said unevenly.

She felt bereft. Alone. A chill wind seemed to slice through her. "Why?" she asked. "Why?"

"Because you don't know me, Alexandra. And because, God help me, I don't know you."

Dear Reader,

Silhouette Desire matches August's steamy heat with six new powerful, passionate and provocative romances.

Popular Elizabeth Bevarly offers *That Boss of Mine* as August's MAN OF THE MONTH. In this irresistible romantic comedy, a CEO falls for his less-than-perfect secretary.

And Silhouette Desire proudly presents a compelling new series, TEXAS CATTLEMAN'S CLUB. The members of this exclusive club are some of the Lone Star State's sexiest, most powerful men, who go on a mission to rescue a princess and find true love! Bestselling author Dixie Browning launches the series with *Texas Millionaire*, in which a fresh-faced country beauty is wooed by an older man.

Cait London's miniseries THE BLAYLOCKS continues with *Rio: Man of Destiny*, in which the hero's love leads the heroine to the truth of her family secrets. The BACHELOR BATTALION miniseries by Maureen Child marches on with *Mom in Waiting*. An amnesiac woman must rediscover her husband in *Lost and Found Bride* by Modean Moon. And Barbara McCauley's SECRETS! miniseries offers another scandalous tale with *Secret Baby Santos*.

August also marks the debut of Silhouette's original continuity THE FORTUNES OF TEXAS with Maggie Shayne's *Million Dollar Marriage*, available now at your local retail outlet.

So indulge yourself this month with some poolside reading— the first of THE FORTUNES OF TEXAS, and all six Silhouette Desire titles!

Enjoy!

Joan Marlow Golan
Senior Editor

Please address questions and book requests to:
Silhouette Reader Service
U.S.: 3010 Walden Ave., P.O. Box 1325, Buffalo, NY 14269
Canadian: P.O. Box 609, Fort Erie, Ont. L2A 5X3

# LOST AND FOUND BRIDE
## MODEAN MOON

SILHOUETTE *Desire*

Published by Silhouette Books

**America's Publisher of Contemporary Romance**

SILHOUETTE BOOKS

ISBN 0-373-76235-6

LOST AND FOUND BRIDE

Copyright © 1999 by Modean Moon

All rights reserved. Except for use in any review, the reproduction or utilization of this work in whole or in part in any form by any electronic, mechanical or other means, now known or hereafter invented, including xerography, photocopying and recording, or in any information storage or retrieval system, is forbidden without the written permission of the editorial office, Silhouette Books, 300 East 42nd Street, New York, NY 10017 U.S.A.

All characters in this book have no existence outside the imagination of the author and have no relation whatsoever to anyone bearing the same name or names. They are not even distantly inspired by any individual known or unknown to the author, and all incidents are pure invention.

This edition published by arrangement with Harlequin Books S.A.

® and TM are trademarks of Harlequin Books S.A., used under license. Trademarks indicated with ® are registered in the United States Patent and Trademark Office, the Canadian Trade Marks Office and in other countries.

Visit us at www.romance.net

Printed in U.S.A.

---

## MODEAN MOON

once believed she could do anything she wanted. Now she realizes there is not enough time in one's life to do everything. As a result, she says her writing is a means of exploring paths not taken. Currently she works as a land title researcher, determining land or mineral ownership for clients. Modean lives in Oklahoma on a hill overlooking a small town. She shares a restored Victorian farmhouse with a six-pound dog, a twelve-pound cat and, reportedly, a resident ghost.

# One

Richard Jordan stood in the shadow of the draperies, but not completely unnoticed. The man behind the massive mahogany desk—the doctor, Richard thought derisively, Dr. Hampton—was aware of him. Although Hampton attempted an attitude of professional detachment, Richard saw the moisture beading on his forehead and upper lip as he gripped the pen in his hand and scrawled tense circles on the folder before him.

The atmosphere in the spacious room was close and stifling. Heavy mahogany furniture filled the room, heavy paneling diminished it, and heavy draperies darkened it still more. No medicinal smells intruded—only those of old wood and lemon oil. Not pleasant scents these; no, the old wood here carried the essence of rot, of wood worms busily destroying the structure behind the facade, and of decadence.

Outside the decoratively barred windows the late-

October sunlight fought its way through the bare limbs of the trees, and a light breeze scattered the fallen leaves across the lawn. Outside, the air was crisp and fresh, promising a harsh winter but beguiling with its gentleness. Richard fought a fleeting impulse to thrust open the windows, in spite of the discreet wiring of the alarm system along the edge of them, and let that breeze into the room. Would that cleanse the air in the room? Could anything cleanse it?

But it was not the doctor behind the desk, or even the room that held his attention. It was the woman. Swathed in a shapeless, long-sleeved garment, she sat on the edge of the chair in front of the desk. The anger that he had felt when he'd first seen her asleep in a room bare of anything except the narrow cot on which she'd lain had not faded. He knew he might never lose the anger, but it had firmed itself into a chilling resolve—to have her released into his care.

Her hair, once shimmering ebony that fell to below her waist, had been cropped close to her head with no thought given to style. Always slender, she now appeared almost skeletal. But it was the sight of her eyes that fed his anger, that had him clutching at the window ledge to keep from lunging across the room. Gone was the sparkle of intelligence and humor that had lit her small features. Her eyes were now two gray smudges in the pallor of her face, without life, without hope, smudges that she turned toward the man behind the desk.

Even her voice had changed—still soft, still low, but without the music of laughter, without the breathless catch of anticipation. Without inflection of emotion, she answered Hampton's questions—the same questions, the same answers Richard had heard the day before.

"What is your name?"

"Alexandra Wilbanks."

"What is your birthday?"

"October 27."

"What day is this?"

"March 15."

"What is your husband's name?"

"I have no husband."

Hampton turned to him and spoke, calling attention to his presence, but the woman did not move.

"As you can see, as I told you yesterday Mr. Jordan, she is completely out of touch with reality."

"Not quite." Richard stepped from his place in the shadows. The answers were wrong for the questions, but they were based in reality—a reality this so-called doctor would have discovered for himself had he ever attempted to help her. Wilbanks, the name under which she had been admitted, was her maiden name. October 27, though not her birthday, was her wedding day. And March 15 was the day his plane had crashed.

Richard walked to her chair and knelt in front of her, willing himself to think of nothing but her and the present moment. He braced his hands on the arms of the chair as he spoke softly.

"Lexi?"

She cocked her head at the sound of his voice and turned her eyes toward him.

"Do you remember me?"

He thought he saw a question in the flatness of her eyes. It was fleeting, and he couldn't be sure whether he had seen it or imagined it, but she looked at him—at the irritation on his cheek where dermal abrasion had finally removed the last of the scars, at the angry red welts still showing on his hand as it rested on the chair arm.

"You came. Before."

He let his breath out in a long, slow exhalation. "Yes. Yesterday." And it had taken all his control not to carry her from this place at that time. All his control to pretend to agree with Hampton that she was where she needed to be. But he had sensed that pretense was necessary for her safety, and he had needed time to prepare for today.

"Would you like to go away with me?"

There. He saw it again, and it wasn't his imagination. A question in her eyes. A ghost of a smile flitted across her features, softening the tight mask of her face.

"They won't let you take me," she said softly. "I'll never be allowed to leave."

His hands tightened on the chair arms, but he kept his voice low and controlled. "Yes. You will."

He straightened and turned to face the man behind the desk. "Send for her things."

Hampton also stood. Richard watched him warily. The man was cool, but not so cool as he wanted to appear: his hands were clenched at his sides. "Perhaps we should send her back to her room while we discuss this."

"No." Richard stepped to the desk. "She doesn't leave my sight again until she walks out of here with me." He picked up the folder on the desk. "And this."

"No."

"These are her records, aren't they?" Richard asked, but he knew the answer. They were. At least a part of them. There probably were more, hidden somewhere.

"Yes. Yes, of course."

"And they would be forwarded to the next physician as a matter of routine."

Hampton's hands clenched again. "Yes."

"Then I see no problem," Richard told him. "But if you don't wish me to take them now, I'm sure you won't object to my calling for a full-scale investigation of your *hospital.*"

Hampton attempted to stare him down, but when that failed, he turned to the intercom unit on his desk. He depressed the lever. "Alexandra is leaving us," he said. "Bring her things to my office."

"Doctor, I should—" The voice of the guardian of the outer office burst through the small speaker before it was muffled and then silenced. "Yes. Immediately," she said in more subdued tones.

When the knock sounded on the door a few minutes later, Richard interposed and opened the door himself. He took the small package from the tight-featured, gray-faced woman and closed the door on her and the outer office.

He looked inside the package. A pair of dark blue lightweight wool slacks. A light blue mohair sweater. A wisp of a bra and matching briefs in ice blue. A pair of Italian sandals.

"Where are her rings?" Richard asked. "Her identification? The rest of her clothes?"

"That's all," Hampton told him. "She came with only the clothes she wore."

Richard muttered an oath as he slammed the garments back into the package, but when he approached the woman in the chair, his actions and his voice were once again gentle. He touched her arm, and she looked up at him blankly.

"Let's go, Lexi."

She stood obediently and let him guide her across the room, through the doorway and into the outer office, while Hampton followed.

The outer office was full of men, as Richard had known it would be, and they were silent, as they had promised him. He turned to look at Hampton, who had paused at the doorway, visibly paler as he recognized the prosecuting attorney standing before his secretary's desk.

"Dr. Wilford Hampton?" the prosecuting attorney asked, but it was a ritual question, requiring no response. "I have a search warrant for this hospital, and an order requiring you to allow your patients to be examined by an independent team of physicians."

"Jordan!" Hampton's voice broke. "You have the records. You said—"

Richard turned a cold smile on the man. "I lied. I wanted to kill you, Hampton, but men living in civilization no longer do that. Instead, I'll break you. And if these men find what I think they will, I'll take great pleasure in seeing you behind bars, where you will no longer be able to control your nefarious empire."

One deputy detached himself from the throng, took the folder and package from Richard and led the way to the outer door. He opened it and waited while Richard guided Lexi, still obedient, unquestioning, an automaton who responded to the slightest pressure on her back, from the prison where she had been kept for the last seven months.

On the top step of the porch, in her first stubborn action since he had come for her, she stopped. He looked down at her. Unaware of him or of the official cars now cluttering the parking lot, she lifted her face to the sun and filled her lungs with the fresh October air. Then she waited, once again obedient, for him to direct her.

The uniformed chauffeur stood at attention by the open passenger door of the limousine as Richard guided Lexi to the car. Then in an act of consideration that Richard had not thought possible from a veritable stranger, he produced a folded blanket and handed it to Richard.

Richard took it, unfolded it, draped it over Lexi's thin shoulders and helped her into the car.

The man who had accompanied them from the clinic took his place in the front seat of the limo, and silently, powerfully, the automobile pulled away from the converted Georgian mansion, glided through now-open gates and sped on its way.

Lexi showed no interest in the interior of the car, or in the autumn scenery along the twenty-five-mile route into the heart of Boston. She sat quietly during the entire drive, not even looking up when the powerful automobile pulled to a stop in the alley outside the service entrance of a hotel.

Richard helped her from the car and looked down at her as she stood shivering beneath the blanket. Her shoes were only slippers, little more than scraps of inexpensive cotton fabric with flimsily reinforced soles. Swearing under his breath, he bent to take her in his arms. She stiffened but made no protest when he touched her.

"I'm going to carry you," he told her. "Don't be alarmed."

But of course she wasn't alarmed, he realized. She tolerated his lifting her into his arms just as she had tolerated everything else for God-only-knew how long with a quiet acceptance. And she weighed almost nothing—a fragile weight that he held easily, but carefully, next to his heart.

The man who had accompanied them from the clinic led the way, across the alley and in through the hotel's service door, to the freight elevator, which a uniformed police officer held open and waiting for them. He gave the guard the folder of records and spoke softly to him before joining Richard and Lexi in the elevator and pushing the button for their floor. When they reached the floor, he led them down the long, carpeted hallway and opened the door of the suite at the end of it, stepping inside after them, but remaining by the door.

Richard settled Lexi on the brocade-covered sofa and stood back, watching her, but she didn't look at him. She stared blankly ahead, toward the window.

He stifled still another oath and turned from the sight of her. A tray of drinks waited on a nearby table, and he crossed to it and splashed a hefty dose of scotch into a crystal tumbler.

The noise was so slight he barely heard it. He turned toward its source. Lexi had shrugged off the blanket and risen to her feet. Now she walked slowly across the room, toward the window. There was a table in front of the window, and on that table, an arrangement of spring flowers—harder than the devil to find at this time of year, Richard had been told, but he had insisted. She bent to the flowers, inhaling their scent. He watched her, unable to take his eyes from her, and unsteadily lifted the glass to his mouth as she touched one slender finger to the bright blue petal of a forget-me-not barely visible for the profusion of Dutch iris and sprays of forsythia.

"Richard."

His name on her lips was the last thing he had expected to hear. It stunned him into immobility. She turned, her eyes enormous, her hands outstretched—pleading with him?—holding him at bay?—her voice a thin, reedy moan. *"Why?"*

As he watched in stunned disbelief, she began crumpling, folding in on herself. By the time he realized what was happening, by the time he tossed the glass away from him, she was falling. By the time he reached her, she lay unconscious on the carpeted floor. He scooped her up, glaring a warning at the deputy, who had also run to her side, and carried her into the adjoining bedroom.

With one hand, he tore back the covers of the bed and laid Lexi on the sheet. Mindful of the man who'd moved to the other side of the open door, he seated himself on the edge of the bed, shielding her from view as he eased the abominable dress from her.

She wore nothing under the dress except a pair of cheap cotton underpants that were much too large for her. She was unmarked, if he could call emaciation unmarked, except for her arms. He touched the arm nearest him. It, like the other, bore the marks of careless injections. But this one still carried the bruise of a healing hematoma, which discolored the skin for several inches above and below the crook of her elbow.

Richard began swearing, silently, viciously. He damned Hampton and his entire staff. He damned his mother, no matter what the truth was. He damned the doctor who had first mentioned Hampton's hospital. And finally he damned himself for his own carelessness, his own stupidity.

He bent over her, sliding his arms around her cautiously, knowing he could crush her with no effort, and held her while his silent tirade continued.

"Mr. Jordan?"

The voice from the doorway was an intrusion he didn't want to deal with. He ignored it, until it came again.

"Mr. Jordan," the man said again, now sounding as though he had stepped into the bedroom. "I don't want to bother you, but it's time. We don't want to jeopardize the case by delaying gathering evidence."

Richard silenced him with a curt nod. "I know." Slowly he drew away from Lexi and covered her with the sheet. He reached for the telephone on the nightstand

and punched out the numbers. The phone at the other end was picked up on the first ring.

"We're here," he said, hearing the hoarseness in his voice. "Mel...I need you."

Dr. Melissa Knapp arrived in only moments—her room was just two doors down the hallway—looking beautifully cool and competent in her tailored suit, with each perfect blond hair caught in the sophisticated coil she wore, and accompanied by a uniformed nurse. His sister-in-law drew her brows together, the only sign of her concern, as she looked at Lexi.

"Leave the room, Richard," she said.

"No."

Melissa managed to get between him and the bed. "Then at least step back," she told him. She put her hands on his shoulders. "Please," she said. "It will be easier. Leave the room."

He compromised. He couldn't leave the room, and he couldn't bear to watch as the nurse produced a syringe. He walked to the window and looked down over the street as the blood samples were drawn, as impersonal hands and eyes examined Lexi. A few minutes later the nurse left and, almost simultaneously, the guard arrived with a photocopy of the hospital records. Then Richard and Melissa were alone with Lexi—the guards gone, the evidence gathered, their part of this day finished.

It seemed like hours later, and they were still alone.

The hotel bedroom was softly lit by the lamp Melissa used as she studied the photocopy of the hospital records. Her eyes had widened when she first began reading, but she made no comment, reading silently, with her entire concentration focused on the file in her hands. The sky outside the window was dark now, the building across the street a darker shadow against it.

And Lexi slept on, unaware of them, unmoving.

"Can't you do anything?" Richard asked in frustration, breaking the silence.

Melissa looked up from the papers. "Not until we know what has already been done," she said. Her voice softened. "It doesn't look good, Richard. Drug treatment like she has apparently received was never proper psychiatric therapy, not in the past, certainly not today, and I want the lab report before I make any decision. I'm afraid, though, that we may be looking at addiction, that it's not going to be a matter of just letting her sleep off the medication."

Richard closed his eyes and leaned back in the chair, swallowing once before he spoke. "What do the records say?"

"Too much," Melissa said. "And not enough."

He shrugged impatiently and lunged to his feet. "Damn it, Mel. Don't play games with me." He looked at the silent figure on the bed. "She's my wife!" With visible control he lowered his voice, speaking insistently. "And it was my money that put her there."

"Do you believe that?" Melissa asked. "Do you really believe that?"

Richard turned from her. "Hell, I don't know."

Sighing, he stuffed his hands into the pockets of his suit pants. "Yes, damn it. And because of an overdraft in an unknown account, I have the bank drafts to prove it." He straightened his shoulders and turned to face the woman. "So tell me, Mel, just exactly what do those papers say."

"Richard—"

"Tell me."

"They say I was the referring psychiatrist."

"But you were with Greg."

"They say that Alexandra admitted herself to the clinic."

"But why?" Richard asked. "She'd left me. She was free."

"Richard. Please don't do this to yourself."

"Why, Mel? Why?"

Melissa stood, but after one hesitant step toward him, stopped. "Her medical records state a history of depression—"

"That's nonsense—"

"Following a...following a self-induced abortion."

He saw her. He heard her voice. But nothing made sense. Lexi. Pregnant? Letting him leave without telling him? That he could believe. Being desperate enough to run away in his absence. That he could believe. But to kill a child, any child, even *his* child. No. Not Alexandra. Please, God, not Alexandra.

The shrill ring of the telephone interrupted them. Gathering the copies close, Melissa hurried to the bedside table before the instrument could ring again. She spoke softly, asking few questions, and replaced the receiver. She turned slowly. "It isn't good. Her med levels are much too high."

Richard faced her silently. The news shouldn't have surprised him. They had discussed addiction as a possibility. But only as a possibility. Now it was reality. A reality he had to confirm by looking at the figure in the bed.

Her eyes were open, watching him.

"Lexi?"

At his sharp intake of breath, Melissa turned, too, until she was standing beside him.

Lexi's head twisted on the pillow, a pale blur against the pale linens. She looked from Richard, to Melissa, then back at Richard. Before he realized her intentions, she scrambled up against the headboard, taking the sheet with her. She felt beneath the cover. She was naked except for the ugly cotton underpants, but she seemed to take no notice of that. She bent her legs, reaching to feel her feet.

"My shoes," she said in a little voice. "Where are my shoes?"

Her shoes, those cheap cotton slippers, had fallen from her feet as he carried her to the bed. They had lain in the middle of the floor until the nurse had picked them up and at Richard's insistence had thrown them in the wastebasket, along with her dress.

Richard dropped to sit on the edge of the bed. "You don't need them any longer. You'll have new ones tomorrow. All you want."

"I want *them!*" She shrank away from him, and Richard heard rising hysteria in her voice. "Please. Let me have them. I'll be good. I promise. I'll be good."

Richard clutched her shoulders, holding her in the bed. "For God's sake, Mel, get the damned shoes."

The moment Melissa thrust the shoes into Lexi's groping hands, all the fight went out of her. She ran searching fingers along the insole of each one, then, clutching them to her, she curled around them and slid back down in the bed and into unconsciousness.

Richard sat dazed beside her, looking at the soiled and pitiful treasure she had fought for. The cotton was worn almost through on the soles, and ragged cardboard protruded from rips in the fabric. But Lexi had fought for them.

*Why?*

Even in sleep, her fingers clutched them, fighting his

attempts to remove them. As gently as possible, though, he did.

He glanced at Melissa, but she shook her head, telling him silently that she understood no more than he did. It was almost as if Lexi had searched them. He ran his fingers over the insoles as she had. The change in texture was slight, so slight he almost didn't notice—an area slightly stiffer than the rest of the backing. The tear in the lining was just one of many, but he found it.

Impatient with the tiny opening, he ripped the lining, exposing a folded piece of cardboard different from the faded gray backing. He unfolded it, and a moan broke from him.

The print was cracked and faded from the constant pressure of her foot. It wasn't dated, but Richard needed no date. He and Lexi had renovated the conservatory of his house in Backwater Bay, Oklahoma, the preceding winter. Together they had selected the furniture and had taken delivery on it the week before he left. The picture he held was a snapshot, not a very good one, but good enough to show him and Mel seated on the floral-covered rattan love seat in the conservatory. His face was turned so that his unmarked profile faced the camera, and they were smiling at each other as they shared one of the few moments of the past months in which they had found any reason to smile.

He handed the picture to Melissa, and she studied it silently.

"Do you know what this means?" he asked.

"Yes." She smiled grimly, the first time she had smiled since entering the room. "It means that Alexandra is very tenacious. It means that she has more spirit than either of us gave her credit for. It means that at least a part of her is still intact, still holding on, in spite of what she's gone through.''

''And it means,'' Richard said, not wanting yet to digest what Melissa had said, ''it means that someone in the house, close enough to us to take that photo, made sure that she got a copy of it.''

''Richard.'' Melissa put her hand on his chest. ''She ought to be in a hospital.''

''No! She's been hospitalized too long. I won't send her back to one, and I won't run the risk of exposing her to the press during the early court proceedings unless it becomes absolutely necessary.''

''Withdrawal will be painful for her.''

Richard closed his eyes and bowed his head. ''I know.''

''And for you.''

''I know that, too.''

He opened his eyes and met Melissa's clear, considering gaze. ''How long?'' he asked.

''Several days at a minimum.''

''And after that?''

Melissa refused to look away from him. ''I can't make any promises.''

He groped for her, like a blind man searching for shelter, and she went into his arms, holding him to her. ''Oh, Richard,'' she murmured. ''My dear, dear Richard. I wish I could tell you, but I just don't know.''

# Two

Her first clear thought was that it was snowing.

The only light came from the windows across the room, and in the gray light of early morning, through the partially opened draperies, she saw great white flakes falling straight down.

Her next thought was that she ached—all over—and the weight of the blankets intensified that ache. Her left arm lay on top of the blankets, held immobile by some sort of brace. She grimaced when she saw the needle, but traced a wary glance up the tube leading from it to an IV bottle suspended from a metal rack.

Was this a hospital?

She doubted it. The blankets were too soft and the room was too large for a hospital. And it was too finely furnished.

She glanced around the room, quietly absorbing impressions of her surroundings. There were two chairs near the windows, and across one of them lay a dark mass. As her eyes became accustomed to the light, she realized that the mass was a man, sprawled in the chair. His long legs stretched out in jeans straining at his thighs, and he'd thrown his dark head back while he slept, making vulnerable a strong throat above a black turtleneck sweater.

"Hello."

Her voice cracked, and it was little more than a hoarse whisper, but he heard her. He awoke immediately—she could tell by the way his body tensed—but he lifted his head slowly, looking toward her, before he rose with an agile grace she thought must be unusual for someone of his size and walked to stand beside her.

For a moment his size intimidated her as he loomed over her. He was tall, well over six feet, or so it looked to her from her position of weakness, with a lean strength that reminded her of danger and darkness.

He switched on the lamp on the bedside table, and soft light pooled over that corner of the room, illuminating her. Illuminating him.

He had an aggressive jaw—that was the only word she could find to describe it—shadowed by a night's growth of beard, or more, a straight nose, slightly longish, and a mouth that just missed being generous and was now fixed in a grim frown. His hair was dark, probably black, but it was difficult for her to be sure in the subdued light. His skin should have been swarthy, she thought, to go with the image he presented. But while it was probably naturally dark, now it was unhealthily pale. Deep grooves ran from each side of his nose to the corners of his mouth, emphasizing the frown. His eyes were dark, too, but now they were red rimmed and shadowed.

*Do I know him?* She felt that she ought to.

She realized that he studied her as intently as she had

studied him, and now he seemed to be searching for something in the depths of her eyes.

"You're awake."

"Yes." She felt trapped in his gaze, caught by questions she couldn't answer. "Have you been here...all night?"

His lips twisted at what could have been a not-too-funny joke that he didn't share with her. "Yes."

His voice was deep...and comforting, or she thought it would be if he ever spoke more than a few syllables.

She broke the mesmerizing spell of his eyes and glanced at her arm. "I don't like needles."

"I know."

Careful of her arm, he seated himself on the edge of the bed. "Now that you're back with us, we'll see about getting that removed."

She had been right about his voice. It caressed her.

"Thank you."

Was it safe to look at him? Surely she could do so now without being captured. She glanced up. He still watched her—intent, cautious, questioning.

"I hate to ask this," she said, "but where am I?"

"We're in a hotel. In Boston."

He didn't sound like a Bostonian. His accent was softer. Southern? Perhaps.

She saw the slight softening of his frown and the gentle inquiry in his eyes. "How do you feel?"

She examined her feelings, wondering for the first time how she came to be here. "Like I've been beaten," she admitted. The thought stunned her. "Have I been?"

His eyes shuttered. "No. Don't you remember?"

Remember? Remember what? Her first clear thought had been that it was snowing.

"Who are you?" she whispered, but even as she

asked, she knew there was a more important question. "Who am I?"

His face could have been chiseled from marble—pale, gray marble. His mouth tightened in a thin line. His eyes lost their warmth.

"Your name is Alexandra Jordan," he told her. "I call you Lexi. You are my wife."

She had a name now, Alexandra Jordan, and an age, twenty-six, a husband and a family. Melissa, *Dr.* Melissa Knapp, was part of that family, married to Richard's brother, Greg, also a doctor. But these were things Lexi had been told in the long, slow weeks of recuperation since she'd awakened to find Richard keeping vigil by her bed, not things she remembered.

She remembered nothing, not even the cause of her strange, debilitating illness, because she couldn't call the fragmented comments that occasionally fell from her lips remembering. She didn't like needles. She was fond of the color blue. She liked seafood and fresh fruit—and spring flowers. At least, she thought those were her feelings. But each time one of those comments slipped from her, Melissa's eyes narrowed, and Lexi felt like a laboratory animal under examination.

And no one had explained the nature of the illness that had robbed her of her memory. Nor would anyone tell her anything about her past other than the basic facts of her identity.

"It's best for you to remember for yourself," Melissa had said, not unkindly but with a determination that told Lexi that arguing would be futile.

And Richard, the dark stranger who was her husband, seemed at times even less approachable than Melissa.

Now they were taking her home. But even as they sat

almost in isolation in the first-class section of the jet that carried them inland from Boston, they had granted her only the general destination. Oklahoma. Lexi had a fragmented concept of that state, dimly calling up pictures of prairie and dust, Indians and teepees, but the terrain she saw from the window of the small plane into which they had transferred at Dallas was anything but flat or dry.

They had flown for miles over mountains—tall hills, Lexi amended mentally. There were no jagged peaks, only timber and rock-covered mounds pushing up from the surface of the earth. And in the center of those hills, seeming to stretch forever from south to north, with great fingers reaching out from it, lay a vast lake.

"What is it called?" Lexi asked.

"Eufaula," Richard said.

"Eufaula." Lexi tried the word experimentally. Yew-fall-lah. "Is it a French name?"

"Creek," he told her. "Indian."

Melissa, seated in a front seat next to the pilot, seemed engrossed in some papers she had carried with her, and Lexi sensed a different mood in Richard from that which had held him locked in silence.

"Was our home built near the lake?" she asked, hesitant, but needing to test that mood.

"Not exactly."

Lexi felt a small stab of disappointment. "Oh."

Richard frowned and leaned closer to her, speaking in a soft, conspiratorial voice hidden from the others by the drone of the single engine. "Why do you sound so deflated?"

"You're always doing that," she said, for the moment not the least intimidated by the man who had complete control over her life. "It isn't fair, you know, for you to expect answers and never give any."

She thought she had destroyed the fragile moment. Richard's lips thinned, and his eyes—they were black, she had long since discovered—bore into her. "Perhaps it isn't," he admitted. "Why were you disappointed, Lexi?"

She had destroyed the moment. "It isn't important," she said.

"You don't know that!"

"No. No, I don't, do I?" Her frustration had been building almost daily, and now she vented it in softly hissed words. "I know nothing but what you choose to tell me. And you choose to tell me very little. Why, Richard? What are you hiding from me?"

Their time in the Boston hotel room even with his frequent absences had done nothing to improve Richard's pallor. Now he seemed to pale even more with her words. He gripped her shoulders with both hands, as though he wanted to shake her, she thought, or—or pull her against the strength of his chest and hold her there with arms that now trembled with the effort of doing neither.

"Why were you disappointed?" he repeated.

His strength was too much for her; his determination was too much for her. "I just—" *What?* It had been so fleeting, she couldn't call it a memory. "I just thought it would be pleasant to live near the water."

He closed his eyes and released a long breath. Then, as though realizing how tightly he held her, he loosened his grip on her shoulders.

"And so you shall," he said.

She looked away from his face in confusion, to where his left hand rested warmly against her, to the raw scars that ran across the back of that hand to be partially hidden beneath the sleeve of his shirt. She had wondered about the scars, had wondered if there was any connection between them and her loss of memory. But this was of her past and therefore a forbidden subject, as were so many, and she had exhausted her small store of energy.

She sighed in defeat and closed her eyes to hide the sheen of tears that gave evidence to it.

"Your answer was important, Lexi."

It was a concession, and she knew she should be grateful for it. "But you won't tell me why?"

"I can't," he said. A note of insistence crept into his voice. "Be patient, even if I sometimes seem to be just the opposite. We have to trust Mel's judgment in this, at least for a while longer."

The plane banked and began circling to land. Richard leaned back in his seat. Taking her hand in his much larger one, he laced his fingers with hers. Lexi glanced out the window, but the rough terrain leaped to meet her. She twisted away from the sight.

Richard was watching her, emotionlessly, and for the moment she didn't mind his scrutiny. The trip had tired her more than she thought possible, but she saw her own exhaustion mirrored in his eyes, in the tight set of his jaw, in the gray cast to his skin. How long had it been since he had slept an entire night? Even though with the coming of dawn he withdrew from her, he was always there for her in the night when she needed him.

She felt a nameless fear rising up to meet her, even as the ground below seemed to. Richard held his hand out to her. Closing her eyes and her mind to that fear, she leaned back against the seat and held on to his hand— her lifeline.

"My God," Lexi said in a shocked whisper.

The drive from the private landing strip had been unremarkable, and in the growing darkness she had only

had impressions of the rough, timbered hillside. A pause
at two stone gateposts and massive iron gates that opened
electronically, even the mass of the house seen dimly
when the car pulled up to the unimposing double front
doors, had not prepared her for the shock that awaited
her inside.

The three of them had climbed a short flight of marble
steps to the wide, rose-colored marble hall that stretched
away on each side of them. Across it, and down two
steps, she saw a massive reception chamber. Twisted Co-
rinthian columns rose to an arched and muraled ceiling.

Lexi looked up at the man beside her. No wonder he
hadn't told her about this. How could he have prepared
her? "Do we *live* here?" she asked.

"Well, well. The weary travelers finally return."

"Greg!"

Lexi heard emotion in Melissa's voice for the first time
as the woman started toward the man approaching them
painfully slowly with the aid of crutches.

"Surprised, Wife, dear? I told you I wouldn't stay in
that damned wheelchair forever."

"But your hands—" Melissa said.

"Forget my hands!"

The man stopped in front of them. He raked his gaze
over Lexi. Should she know him? She thought she saw
a flash of recognition in his eyes. She knew he was Richard's brother—half brother—and she did see a resemblance, although he was not as tall, not as lean as the
man who stood beside her with tension stiffening his
body even as he draped his arm over her shoulder. But
know him?

"So you're the woman who finally trapped my
brother?"

Lexi flinched from the bitterness in the man's voice.

"That's enough, Greg."

Richard spoke softly, but Lexi heard the implied command, and apparently Greg did, too. His face twisted into a smile.

"Of course, Richard. We wouldn't want to upset anyone, would we?" He shifted his weight on his crutches and turned. "Your oh-so-efficient housekeeper has a light supper waiting for you, as well as a list of telephone messages. At least six of them are from your agent."

"Alexandra is tired," Richard said, interrupting Greg and tightening his arm on her shoulder, urging her to turn. "I'll take her to her room now, but I'll see you in the library in a few minutes."

This time the command was not implied. Lexi turned, grateful to be leaving a scene she couldn't begin to understand, and let Richard guide her up the staircase.

Upstairs, although the floor of the hallway was polished oak, not marble, Oriental runners and arrangements of massive furniture carried out the oppressiveness of the first floor.

Lexi cast a covert glance at the man walking silently beside her. Who was he? She thought she had seen all facets of him during the long weeks in Boston, from gentleness to impassive detachment, but never had she seen him exercise authority with such a sure knowledge of his right to do so. Could it be the house? No. She discarded that thought immediately. If anything, the house was a mere reflection of him, not the other way around. And he seemed to belong. She could see that now. From his erect carriage and the proud tilt of his head to the well-tailored suit and Italian shoes, he fit his surroundings. While she...?

She knew nothing about him—nothing more than she had known the morning she awoke to find a stranger beside her bed—a stranger who told her he was her husband.

*Her husband.*

Melissa, omniscient Melissa, had finally told Richard that Lexi was well enough to return home. Had she also told him that she was well enough to resume her conjugal duties?

Lexi stumbled, and immediately Richard turned, steadying her. She looked up at him, half expecting him to have read her thoughts, but there was wary concern in his eyes, nothing more. She felt the pressure of his hands on her arms, felt the strength inherent in those hands, and the gentleness. Would it be a duty? she wondered. Had it been only that in the past? Or had it been much, much more?

She offered him a tentative smile in apology for her clumsiness, and her thoughts, and he rewarded her by the softening of the concern in his eyes.

"Are you all right?"

No, she wasn't. As she stood in the dim light of the alien hallway, with Richard looming darkly over her, she was more aware of that fact than she had been since her first moment of panic.

She didn't know how she would have answered him in the past. She didn't know how he expected his wife to answer him now. She only knew the irony of his words.

"Silly question, Richard," she said, throwing her head back so that she could meet his penetrating gaze. "You must know that I'm terrified."

He almost smiled. She was sure of that.

"Of what, Lexi?" he asked, still holding her. "Of my house, of my family, of what you can't remember? Of me?"

"Yes."

Even as she said the word, she knew it was not the truth. Richard's eyes lost all traces of warmth, and he dropped his hands to his side.

"Not—not of you," she said softly. "But of what—what you expect from me. And maybe of what I expect from myself."

"And if I were to tell you that I expect nothing from you?"

"But you won't tell me that, will you?" she asked.

He shook his head slowly. "No."

He took her arm, and beneath all the layers of fabric, her flesh felt and came alive at his touch. It wasn't fear, Lexi told herself, so much as it was an awareness of the power he held over her—physically, emotionally, even financially. No. Not fear. Not once since awakening to find him beside her bed had she feared him. Perhaps she should, she thought fleetingly. Perhaps one day she would. She pushed back those unwanted thoughts, not knowing what had called them forth and not wanting to examine the chill that had accompanied them.

The room he took her to was at the end of the long hallway. Opening a recessed door, Richard moved back to let her enter first.

She stepped into a room large enough to have been overpowering had it been furnished as the reception hall and hallway were. But it wasn't. Soft lamps had been lit, casting warm circles of light throughout the room. Decorated in shades of blue, the room was delicate but not cloyingly so.

Lexi shrugged out of her coat, with Richard's assistance, and while he dropped it onto a nearby French chaise, she surveyed the room, letting her smile play across her features.

Apart from the chaise, she saw no other French influence. The tables were English of Hepplewhite design, and their dark surfaces gleamed in the subdued light. The upholstered pieces were substantial, but not ungainly. Two club chairs and a matching sofa in softly tailored oyster white linen fronted a fireplace with a delicately veined white marble mantel.

Across the room, an alcove with two walls of windows and a third of French doors, all covered with tailored silk draperies, sheltered an overlarge, king-size bed.

She turned to find Richard watching her reaction.

"Is this better?" he asked.

"Oh, yes." Even knowing this must be his room, too, even seeing how he seemed to belong in these surroundings, she couldn't keep the relief from her voice. "I was half expecting gargoyles and griffons on the ceiling and bedposts."

"No. No monsters, Lexi. That's something you won't tolerate."

Then, perhaps thinking he had said too much, he half turned from her. "Your bath and dressing rooms are through there," he said, nodding toward a door on a railed landing raised a few steps from the floor of the room. "I think you'll find everything you need. I'll bring you a tray when I come back upstairs. I shouldn't be too long, but you'll probably have time for a bath before I return."

"Richard?"

He completed his turn, walked to a door near the hallway, and opened it.

"I've had my things moved into the adjacent room," he said. "There is a key for the hall door, but I'd appreciate it if you would leave this door partially open so that I can hear you if you need me in the night."

"Richard?" She watched him in confusion. He had reverted to impassive detachment. Polite, impersonal, he was treating her like a dependent stranger while she had questions spinning through her mind. He'd had his things moved. He *belonged* in this room. And while she wasn't brave enough—didn't know him well enough—to ask him to stay, there were questions she had to ask.

"We shared this room?"

He paused in the doorway. "Yes."

"And that bed?"

His glance flicked toward the bed and back to her without revealing anything. "Yes."

"Were we happy here?" she persisted. "Did we love each other?"

"Lexi." His voice held a soft groan. "Why are you asking me?"

"Who else can I ask?" She walked to his side. Hesitantly she placed her hand on his arm. "You tell me this is my home, but I can't remember. You tell me you are my husband. I don't want to hurt you, but I can't remember that, either. Can't you give me at least this much?"

"And you'd believe me?"

She gazed up at him, pleading. "I'd have to, wouldn't I?"

"If I told you that you loved me beyond reason, and the two of us were happier here than any two people had a right to be, you'd believe me?"

She wanted to. Oh, how she wanted to. But she saw the flash of pain in his eyes, hastily banked, when he spoke.

"Or if I told you that you feared me, that you hated this place, that you only waited for a chance to escape, would you believe that?"

She felt his arm tense beneath her hand.

"Why are you doing this?" she whispered. "Why won't you tell me?"

He lifted her hand from his arm, holding it between both of his—safe? imprisoned? she wondered—before he released it.

"You have the answers, Lexi. Whatever they are, you have to discover them for yourself."

# Three

The sound of rain hitting against the windows in irregular, rapid bursts dragged Lexi from sleep. Through partially opened eyes, she noted the dim light in the strangely familiar room and snuggled back into the down pillows with a sense of sleepy satisfaction. It was morning. She had slept the night through, unawakened by disturbing dreams or nightmares that refused to stay in her memory, unawakened by the vague yet demanding longings that sometimes gripped her and held her for sleepless hours.

"Of all the months of the year, I think January must have the most miserable weather."

Lexi's eyes flew open. Between the bed and the French doors stood a slender woman with stylish, short silver hair. The woman wore a dark green velvet dressing gown and looked completely at home in Lexi's bedroom.

"It's later than it seems," the woman continued reflectively. "The storm has darkened the sky. Without a doubt the rain will turn to ice before noon."

Lexi, fully awake now, scooted up against the rose-wood headboard, pulling the blanket with her. The hall door was locked. She had watched Richard turn the key the night before. She glanced across the room. Richard's door stood open.

"Oh, he's downstairs writing in his office," the woman said. "He has been for hours. He spent half his childhood telling his little stories. It is so nice he finally found an outlet for his obsession."

She walked to the bed and seated herself on the edge of it. "I wanted to visit with you while he was busy. He was in such a foul mood when he telephoned weeks ago from Boston. I wanted to resolve at least one thing before I saw him again."

The woman was much older than Lexi had first thought. Though she wore carefully applied, tasteful makeup, she had been unable to hide the network of deep lines fanning out from her dark brown eyes or from her thin, rose-glossed lips.

"I truly wanted to like you, Alexandra. You bear such a stunning resemblance to my niece."

Lexi submitted to the woman's brief, intense scrutiny with growing irritation. She was an amnesiac, not a lab-oratory animal who had no feelings. She could have—would have—demanded that a stranger leave her room, but who in this house *was* a stranger? And who had been given the right to come and go at will?

"You really don't remember, do you?"

Had there ever been any doubt of that? Lexi wondered, but a stubbornness she had not realized she possessed refused to let her answer the woman's question, just as it refused to let her ask the woman's identity.

"Oh, well," the woman said, rising gracefully from the bed. "Perhaps it's for the best, after all."

She crossed to a small table and opened its one drawer. "Richard seemed to think that I knew something about these," she said. "Naturally I was disturbed by his unfounded accusations, disturbed enough that I had to do something. And where better to look than where it all began?"

She closed her fist over something she took from the drawer and walked back to the side of the bed. Lexi watched silently, willing the woman to end her cryptic comments and tell her, straight out, whatever she had come to say.

"They weren't hard to find, not once I decided where to search. They were just stuffed in the back of a drawer, where any thief could have found them.

"If I were you, I wouldn't tell Richard how careless you were with them," she said, taking Lexi's hand and pressing two rings into her palm.

Lexi stared at the wide, filigreed gold band and the sapphire and diamonds in an antique setting that complemented it. When she raised her head with a question already forming on her lips, she found that the woman had crossed the room.

Standing in the doorway to Richard's adjoining room, she lifted one delicately arched eyebrow. "And, Alexandra," she said with a trace of condescension in her well-modulated voice, "welcome home."

The night before, the rose-colored bathroom with its marble fixtures had seemed just another indication of the oppressiveness of the house. After a night's sleep, however, Lexi was able to look at the room with new eyes, able to see the beauty in it, and able to wonder, Had she been accustomed to such wealth?

But the clothes in the vast closets, although too large, seemed suited to her. Just as the rings—although she found them, too, a little large once she was no longer able to resist slipping them onto her finger—seemed to belong on her hand.

She wore the rings, testing the feel of them but refusing to give in to the speculation they aroused in her, while she pondered the question of what one wore to breakfast when one lived in a museum. Not one of the several pairs of jeans she found neatly folded in a drawer, she was at enough of a disadvantage already, and not a dress—not for breakfast at home no matter how *unhumble* home was. She compromised with a pair of softly tailored peach-colored wool slacks, a coordinated mohair sweater and comfortable low-heeled shoes.

She felt somewhat like a little girl playing dress-up, but the three-way, full-length mirrors dispelled that image. Her size and the strangely disturbing short, curling hairstyle she now wore conspired to give her the appearance of a gamine. But her eyes held secrets that gave lie to that impression—secrets they wouldn't reveal, even to her.

She was a stranger to herself. As everyone she had met was a stranger to her. As everyone she would meet until this mental blackout was ended would be a stranger to her. And it was a mental blackout. Melissa had made sure she understood that: there was no physical reason, now, for her not to remember.

She found herself twisting the rings on her finger and reluctantly, knowing it was only partially for their protection, drew them from her hand and tucked them into a deep pocket of the slacks.

Realizing she was only postponing the inevitable, Lexi lifted her chin and straightened her shoulders. If this was her home, she wouldn't hide in the bedroom; if this was her family, she wouldn't cower from them, no matter how foreboding they might seem.

Maybe.

Heading downstairs, Lexi sighed with relief when she found the breakfast room. Here, as in her bedroom, someone had banished the gloom. Sheer Austrian curtains covered floor-to-ceiling windows against which the rain spat, but even the foul weather couldn't dispel the charm of the graceful furnishings and the delicate marble fountain set in the bow of one windowed wall. Maybe this house could be—had been—a home, after all.

She pushed through a heavy door and entered an institution-size kitchen.

A fiftyish woman, with neat gray hair caught in a severe bun and wearing an equally neat gray dress over her stolid figure, raised her head from the recipe file on the table in front of her. Her look of surprise quickly turned to barely disguised dismay.

"Mrs. Jordan!"

Lexi stopped hesitantly just inside the doorway. Was this someone else she was supposed to know?

The woman rose from her chair. "Mr. Jordan said you would probably sleep quite late. He told me not to disturb you. But if you had rung me, I would have had your tray brought to you."

Lexi felt a smile quirking her lips as well as a quick stab of frustration. "I'm afraid no one explained the system to me."

"Oh." The woman seemed nonplussed for a moment, and her glance darted around the kitchen before returning to Lexi's face. "I'm sorry. We tend to forget. I—we— I'll be happy to show you how it works. It's tied in with the telephones."

"Thank you," Lexi said. "I would appreciate that." She glanced at the pile of recipe cards and at the well-used oak kitchen table. "I wonder if I might have some coffee."

"Of course." The woman stacked the cards into a neat pile. "You just go on into the breakfast room, and I'll bring it right out."

A dismissal? As polite as it had been, the woman's response had all the earmarks of a firm dismissal.

In only a matter of moments the woman came through the doorway into the breakfast room carrying a tray. Lexi turned from the window where she had been staring out into the rain.

"You can't see the lake this morning because of all the rain," the woman said, setting the tray on the cherry table that would seat ten comfortably. "But it's sure to be roiling and peaking."

Lexi released the curtain and let it drop back into place. "Can we usually see the lake from here?"

The woman looked at her curiously. "Of course."

*Was our home built near the lake?*

*Not exactly.*

Why had Richard said that? She shook her head and walked to the table. A silver coffeepot and one delicate cup waited for her. No cream. No sugar. But then, she didn't need cream and sugar. She looked up at the woman, who was watching her, almost anxiously, from a position by the door.

"I'm—I'm Eva Handly," the woman said reluctantly. "My husband Jack—he met you at the landing strip last night—have worked for Mr. Jordan for years, here, and—and for you.''

Lexi sighed and nodded her head in acknowledgment of the introduction. "Thank you, Mrs. Handly," she said softly. "I really do hate to have to ask."

For a moment the woman seemed to warm toward her, but only for a moment. "I'll have your breakfast out in a few minutes."

"No," Lexi said. "This is all I want."

"Young Mrs. Knapp has already given me my orders," Mrs. Handly said firmly before leaving the room.

Melissa's idea of a suitable breakfast left a lot to be desired, Lexi thought later. It was suitable, she supposed for a farm hand or a laborer, but there was no way she could eat all of the beautifully prepared meal. There was no way she wanted to try.

Had Melissa always been so arbitrary? Maybe she had. Maybe only now was Lexi beginning to resent it. But surely the decision of whether she wanted breakfast was one she was capable of making for herself.

She was pushing the food around on her plate, wondering what she would do with the rest of the morning, when Richard walked into the room.

She started guiltily as she looked up at him, and abandoned her immediate halfhearted fight against the pleasure she felt at seeing him. He looked almost rested, and he was dressed casually in faded jeans and another of his innumerable long-sleeved turtleneck sweaters that set off the strength in his arms and shoulders and threw his dark features into harsh relief. He looked at home here, at ease with his surroundings, and although he gave her another of his wary smiles, he seemed almost happy to see her, too.

"Eva told me you were here," he said in the com-

forting voice she had relied upon for so many days before
she had begun to notice his detachment, that she still
relied upon when he came to her in the long hours of the
night. He drew out the chair next to her and seated himself. "Did you rest well?"

"Yes." She dared a hesitant smile. "Did you?"

This time his smile was less wary. "Surprisingly
well." He glanced at the plate in front of her. "Don't let
me keep you from your breakfast."

Lexi glanced at the mountain of food remaining and
surrendered to a tiny grimace. "Please do." She gestured
toward the silver pot. "Would you like some coffee?"

He shook his head. "I've had more than I need already
this morning."

She poured a little more of the still steaming liquid
into her cup and sipped at it tentatively. She hated to
break the mood between them, but then, what was the
mood?

"What now?" she asked.

He reached with his strong, long-fingered, unscarred
hand and traced the path of a feathered curl against her
cheek. Beneath his touch, her cheek seemed to tingle, to
throb almost painfully as though too long denied the sus-
tenance of blood, of life. Lexi caught her lower lip between her teeth as she watched his dark eyes follow the
path of his hand and then look to hers questioningly.

"I thought I'd give you a tour of the house so that you
won't be completely lost," he said at last. "If you would
like."

"Oh, yes," she said, not wanting to be relegated back
to the solitude of her room, and not wanting, yet, to be
deprived of Richard's company. "I'd like that very
much."

* * *

Richard started the tour with the adjacent room, a dining room that dwarfed the proportions of the breakfast room. Lexi seated herself on the arm of a chair and stared around it pensively.

The room was heavy. That was the only word for it. Heavy Spanish furnishings. Heavy drapes that blocked out all outside light. Flickering wall sconces, meant to represent candlelight, only added to the gloom.

She couldn't hide her shiver as she felt the walls, the wooden-paneled ceiling and the furnishings all closing in on her.

Richard leaned against the sideboard with his long legs crossed casually, though he wasn't at ease. Why did he think he had to pretend to be?

"Would it help if I told you your very first words to me over a year ago when I brought you to this house?"

Lexi felt her breath catch. Warily she turned to him.

"You said, 'My God, do we *live* here?'"

"But that's what I said—"

"Last night," he finished for her. He abandoned his casual slouch against the sideboard and walked to her side, looking down at her. "You don't like this room, Lexi. You never have. And you don't have to worry about hurting my feelings by telling me. I don't like it, either."

"Does this mean—" She realized she had been holding her breath and expelled it slowly. "Does this mean you've decided to talk to me?"

"About some things," he admitted. "You've got to understand that I know no more about how to help you than you do. When Mel said that we should tell you nothing, that we should let all your knowledge come from your subconscious, I had to agree with her. She is a doctor. She is trained in these matters. But I've given a lot of thought to what you said yesterday, and while I still agree with Mel, at least in part, I see no reason why you should be kept completely in the dark.''

He stared into her eyes with an intensity that would have stripped secrets from her soul, if she'd had any to share, and a chill claimed his features. "I want to know—*have* to know—the truth. And so do you. If this is the only way to learn what that truth is, so be it."

Lexi shifted on the chair arm, away from this suddenly frightening stranger, and when she did, she felt the rings in her pocket pressing against her thigh. In a nervous gesture she was barely conscious of, she began massaging the base of her ring finger with her thumb as she remembered the cryptic words of the woman who had given them to her.

"Richard, does Melissa—do you..." Lexi fumbled for the words, not wanting to believe that he could think so, but knowing she had to ask. "Is there some doubt? Did you think that by not telling me anything, that I might, somehow, slip and prove that I really do remember?"

Richard captured her hand in both of his and stilled her nervous movement. "Why do you ask that?"

Lexi swallowed once and then met his eyes. "I had a visitor in my room when I woke up this morning."

"Who?" The pressure of his hands tightened on hers.

"A woman. Silver hair. Very...stylish. She didn't tell me who she was. I wouldn't ask."

Richard dropped her hand and twisted away, but not before she saw the flash of a pain so old, so deep, she wondered how he bore it. "Damn her!"

It wasn't an answer, but Lexi sensed that it was the only answer she was going to get. Should she tell him about the rings? Maybe she should, she admitted, but she wasn't ready to face a confrontation with this man about whether or not to wear the visible symbol that she belonged to him—*or he to her,* a small voice whispered—not when his face had tightened into a dark scowl that hid all the kindness she'd thought he possessed. Perhaps she could have found the courage to do so if that glimpse of his pain had remained. But now his black eyes reflected an even blacker anger.

"Your door was locked?"

"Yes. I checked it after she left. She left through your room."

"I'm sorry." He placed his hand on the side of her head, almost reluctantly caressing a wayward curl, and let it slide down until it rested on her shoulder. "It shouldn't have happened. It won't happen again."

Lexi looked at his scarred hand resting against soft, peach-colored wool and felt the warmth of his touch seeping through to her. She fought the urge to rest her cheek against his hand and fought the urge to ask him about the scars. She looked up at him, but he had seen the direction of her gaze. He lifted his hand from her and stuffed it into the pocket of his jeans.

"Who was she, Richard?" Lexi asked, when she realized he was lost in bitter thoughts of his own.

He sighed. "My mother. You'll see her again at lunch."

The weather prevented them from going outside, so Richard confined their tour to the house. But even after they had passed through several rooms his mood did not lighten, only settled into one that was slightly less grim.

There were rooms they didn't enter: Greg's ground-floor bedroom next to the basement-to-attic antique elevator that had been restored to accommodate his wheelchair, the bedrooms occupied by Richard's mother,

Helene, and Melissa at the opposite end of the second floor and a locked door beyond Lexi's suite that Richard explained was a sunroom undergoing renovation and not safe for her to enter.

There were places Lexi didn't like, which she had suspected there would be: the reception hall, a massive game room on the ground floor with its walls hung with mounted trophies and its floor covered with the tanned hides of long-dead animals; and, surprisingly, the narrow service stairs leading from the second-floor servants' quarters, down which she had to force herself to follow Richard.

There were also rooms she found delightfully inviting. Yet only in the conservatory, a glass-walled and roofed structure appended to the east wing of the house, did she feel she could be truly at home. But they only paused in the doorway, looking in at the heated pool and a virtual jungle of tropical plants before Richard led her away.

And throughout the tour, with a recital stripped of emotion or inflection, Richard told her of the history of the house. He had not lied to her about the lake, he told her eventually. The lake was a relative newcomer, only having been impounded forty years or so ago, while the house had sat on its mountaintop for half again that long. The house had been built by an oilman and land speculator for his mistress and her small daughter by a previous liaison. They had lived here until the oilman's death in the crash of a private plane enroute to a west Texas oil field.

Lexi tried to see the house through the eyes of the woman who had lived in isolated splendor, kept by but not married to a man who had lavished such wealth on her, or through the eyes of the child. Had the girl slid down the banister of the formal staircase or skated along the marble hallways? Or had she been a shy child, awed by her surroundings?

"He must have loved her very much," she said.

"Not enough to leave his wife and son and marry her," Richard said abruptly. "Not enough to cut out even a few acres of land from his holdings and deed this or any other property to her. Not even enough to make provisions for her in his will."

"What happened?"

"His wife evicted them. On the day of his funeral, she fired the entire household staff and replaced them with employees of her choice, who watched while the woman and child packed their clothes. Grandmother wasn't altogether ungenerous," Richard said dryly. "She did give them one of the cars so they could leave."

"Your grandmother?" Lexi asked.

Richard nodded. "Although she was about as ungrandmotherly as you can imagine. She didn't look it, but she was as tough as a drill stem. She'd had to be. She'd worked side by side in the oil fields with my grandfather. But she was as brittle as an *old* drill stem, and she never forgave him for spending *her* money on *that woman*."

"What happened to *that woman?*" Lexi asked, appalled by the betrayal both women must have felt.

"I'm not sure," Richard told her. "There was speculation that she must have stashed away some money, or jewelry, because it was several years before anyone heard from her, and then it was in the form of a lawsuit claiming she had been pregnant at the time of the old man's death and that her child should share in his estate. For years the only version I heard was my grandmother's. While I'm sure she was biased, she swore there could be no child, that my grandfather had been incapable of producing another. Even if there was," he said, shrugging off some heavy, unseen weight, "it didn't do much good. The case was settled before trial, probably not pleasantly."

They had come almost full circle in their tour. With gentle pressure on her arm, Richard guided her into a drawing room. He walked to the walnut mantel and stared at the logs stacked in the cold fireplace. Lexi sank down uneasily onto the edge of the overstuffed sofa and watched as he sorted through memories, knowing he must be debating how much to tell her, knowing but not knowing how she knew, that he'd much rather keep this private than share with anyone.

"The house sat here for years, not lived in except by a staff that waxed and polished and dusted it, until my father was in his late twenties and met and married a beautiful woman, a woman no one seemed to know anything about but for whom my grandmother took an instant dislike.

"So my father brought his bride here, although technically it was still my grandmother's property. His bride loved the place, preferring it, she told him, even in its isolation, to the amenities of any city."

Richard's hands clenched but he continued speaking in a calm, reflective voice. "She bore my father a son and swore her undying devotion. Until the day my grandmother found out she was the daughter of *that woman,* the child who had been raised in this house, and swore she would not tolerate her under this roof for even one more night.

"The house, as well as control over most of the estate, was still in my grandmother's hands. Once again, the only version I heard for years was hers, but whatever was said, the result was that my mother left—"

He didn't hear Lexi's small gasp of dismay. Still staring into the logs, he might just as well have been talking to them as to her, she thought.

"She left my father. She left me."

Lexi thought of all the times he had comforted her, holding her without passion through the long hours of the night. Her heart went out to him in his need for comfort, but she sensed he would resent sympathy. She wasn't sure how he would react to anything she offered.

She walked to his side and tentatively placed her hand on his arm. "But she's with you now."

Richard turned to her. His eyes were opaque, and she wasn't sure he really saw her. "Helene is with Greg," he said. "The son she had with the man she married indecently soon after divorcing my father."

He shook his head, clearing his thoughts, and then rubbed at his forehead. "I didn't want to come here, Lexi. The years I spent here as a child weren't particularly happy ones. But there was a time in our lives when we needed privacy." He smiled grimly and looked around the room. "And this place can certainly supply that."

"Have you..." Lexi hesitated, not wanting to say anything that would cause Richard to close himself still farther away from her. "Have you told me this before?" she asked softly.

"No," he admitted. "At least, not all of it. And perhaps I should have."

His eyes, no longer opaque, once again met hers. They were seeking answers, she knew, as they called to her, just the same as she was.

Richard moved abruptly, shattering the tie between them. "It's almost time for lunch," he said. "Do you need to go upstairs for a few minutes to freshen up?"

Lexi tried to mask her sigh of disappointment with a quick nod. "Yes, please."

He was visibly withdrawing from her, and there was nothing she could do to stop him.

"Can you find your way back to your room?" he asked.

Even if she could stop him, could bring his attention back to now, back to her, *should* she?

"Yes. Of course."

"Fine. I'll see you at lunch, then. Half an hour. The family will be waiting."

He nodded abruptly and glanced toward the door. Suddenly he reminded her of a still-ferocious-yet-trapped-and-vulnerable animal. Surely not. Not Richard—her strength, her one link to sanity in the confusion of her life.

# Four

The storm only threatened for the remainder of the day, but shortly after midnight ice arrived. Richard turned in his bed as the first brittle shards hit the window and the Spanish tile roof.

Lexi would be cold.

A moan rose from the lake as the wind whipped over it.

She had never acclimated even to the early spring at Backwater Bay, and he knew from the past that winter pierced her with its gray chill.

Once he would have held her. Once he would have warmed her. Once he would have thought she welcomed him.

Now all he could be sure she wanted from him was comfort when the nightmares ambushed her.

Nightmares. No longer the torture of her body crying out for the drugs that scum of a doctor had foisted on her. Nightmares she couldn't, or wouldn't, talk about. Nightmares that brought her into his arms before she fully awakened from the terror, and kept her there, trembling and needing him, at least for a few minutes.

He glanced at the utilitarian travel clock on the stand beside his bed. Three in the morning. Three, and he lay sleepless, restless and needing in his own way, while Lexi slept soundlessly in the room next door in what had been their bed. She'd slept completely through the night before. Maybe she'd do so again. Maybe the need for his all-night vigils would soon be a thing of the past.

Like the love she had once professed to feel for him.

But then, that love had never really existed except in his mind.

He turned on his back and closed his eyes, listening to the ice beating against the windows. Lexi wasn't the only one who was cold; he was, too, in ways few would understand. Cold to his very core.

He shouldn't have told her the pathetic story of his family's loyalties and lies this morning. Once he started, though, he hadn't found a way to stop. Yes. Yes he had. He'd stopped before telling her of the biggest betrayal of all—the one that had left him wishing this last mission had finished the job of killing him.

Trained by weeks of watching, waiting, listening, he heard her whimper and then moan.

No, she wouldn't sleep this night through.

He reached for the soft cotton sweats he kept beside the bed. In the dark he couldn't see the scars that covered his arm and shoulder, but the ravaged flesh was all too obvious to touch. Quickly he covered himself. No scars for Lexi. That was something else she wouldn't tolerate. *Now his body is as scarred as his soul.* The voice he heard in his mind, taunting him, wasn't hers, but the message was. It was one he'd been waiting for since the first time she'd seen him kill a man.

Her room lay in darkness except for the glow of a small, silk-shaded lamp near the fireplace and the embers of a dying fire. At some point in this sleepless night, he must have dozed, because he hadn't heard her move. Now Lexi lay curled into a corner of the sofa, almost lost in the jumble of pillows and blankets she had dragged from the bed.

Richard stood looking down at her. She'd rejected his bed as she'd rejected him. Her pain now wasn't physical; Mel had assured him of that. And whatever gripped her in the dead of night was something she couldn't or wouldn't share with him. So why did he put himself through the torture of holding her through her nightmares, remembering and needing her, only to be pushed away when her weakness had passed? Only to hate himself for his own weakness in still wanting her.

Lexi turned restlessly, tugging the blanket more securely around her shoulders as a log crumbled in the fireplace, sending light dancing out to reflect back at him from the antique sapphire and diamonds she wore on her left hand.

Her rings.

Rings he had not seen since he left her here, in this room, last March and went off to die in that hell-hole of a jungle hospital.

Rings Hampton swore she had not brought with her to the hell-hole of a hospital *she* had found.

Rings that were the solid symbol of the promise he had made to love and cherish—and protect—this woman who was his wife.

She moaned again as the nightmare drew her more

deeply into its web. Richard seated himself carefully beside her, not yet touching her. Not yet waking her.

Not yet demanding to know where she had found the rings.

She came awake as always, sitting up abruptly with her mouth open in a silent scream and her eyes focused on something he suspected even she did not see.

"Lexi," he said softly, as he had night after night.

She turned toward his voice and then, as always, reached for him, allowing him to take her in his arms, holding him as tightly as he held her, trembling but not crying, not speaking.

"Tell me," he said, equally softly, as he had night after night, knowing that her dreams must hold the key to unlock her memory. "What did you see?"

She shuddered and released her grasp on him, but she didn't pull away. Not yet.

"Telephones," she said. Her voice caught on an indrawn breath. "Miles of them. All with their cords severed and dangling. And stairs. Dark, narrow stairs going down and down and down."

Richard closed his eyes briefly. Some memory of the dream was an improvement, wasn't it? Even if it had no apparent meaning. He smoothed his hands across her back, holding her safe against the night until he felt awareness tightening her body, until he felt her drawing away.

He released her but didn't move from his place on the sofa beside her. She sat up, easing her hands from him, clasping them tightly against her chest as she rocked, only slightly, back and forth.

"Talk about it," he prompted in his quiet, nonthreatening, nighttime voice. Mel had insisted this was important; that while the horror was fresh in Alexandra's mind was the best, perhaps the only time to recover her memories. "Tell me what you saw."

Lexi stilled her restless motion, but she didn't unlock her hands.

"That's all," she said. She drew in a shaky breath. "Telephones and stairs." She coughed out a bitter laugh. "But I suppose that's better than nothing." She looked up at him, and he saw the glitter of unshed tears in her eyes. "And it was dark. So dark. Dark. Dark. Dark..."

He heard the rising hysteria in her voice and reached to calm her. He didn't take her in his arms—the time for that had passed—but placed his hand on her shoulder. No matter the havoc it played with his own tightly drawn needs, this had seemed to calm her always before, to center her in the here and now. This time it didn't. She raised her arm, shrugging off his touch.

"Why, Richard?" She asked the same question she'd asked the day he brought her out of that hell-hole, but not in the same small voice. Now he heard frustration in her demand, and the same anger he felt when he asked himself that question.

*Why, Lexi? Why did you abandon me when I needed you so much? Why couldn't you have lived the charade of our marriage just a little longer? Why did you betray the trust, the love, the dreams I had shared with you? And how in God's name did you manage to do this to yourself?*

"But of course you won't answer me, will you?" For a moment, she turned her anger on him, then dropped back against the pillows with a resigned sigh. "No. Foolish me. Mel says..."

Lexi caught her hand to her mouth almost in time to hold back a sob, and once again firelight glittered from antique gemstones, reminding him of questions *he* needed answered.

"The rings, Lexi?" he asked.

Lexi glanced in startled surprise at the rings on her finger, then closed her other hand over them—hiding them? protecting them?

"They are mine, then?"

*Hers?* Of course they were hers. They had been hers until the day she abandoned them. But where? And how had she once again claimed them? "Where were they?"

"Other than the clothes in the closet, there's nothing of me in this room," she said, not answering his question. "I searched this afternoon. There's not a note, an address, a charge slip—nothing."

He nodded, holding tightly to his patience, willing her to continue and prove to him that she had not added another lie to all that had gone before. "I know. I looked, too, when I returned."

She glanced at him sharply—Returned? From where? And when?—but let his slip of words pass. "Yet you can ask me about the rings."

A blast of ice assaulted the windows and rattled the French doors in the alcove that sheltered the bed. Lexi shivered, and Richard jerked to his feet, away from her. How could she do this? How could she always deflect his anger and manage to turn it into guilt? *Because she didn't want to marry you,* the too-vocal voice in his mind taunted. *You knew it then. You know it now.*

"The rings, Lexi," he said.

She tugged at the rings, freeing her finger from them. "I'm tired of playing Melissa's mind games. I'm tired of being forced to answer questions you already know the answers to. You can answer questions…you proved that today. So why, now, are you doing this to me?"

She held them out to him. "Take them."

He looked down at the antique rings in the palm of her graceful hand, and all the desolation of the past months washed over him. She was abandoning him all over again. He'd not been able to do anything about her abandonment the first time, but this time—oh, yes—this time at least was within his control.

He closed his hand over hers, wrapping the rings securely within her fist. "You have them," he said. "While you are in my house, you will wear them."

He heard her small gasp of shock. She'd always known he was a violent man—wasn't that what had sent her running—so why, now, did her reaction to him still have the power to wound him?

He thrust her hand from him. "Wear them," he repeated. "And you will tell me where they were."

Lexi struggled up from the sofa. With quick, angry jabs she returned the rings to her finger, then fisted her hand and looked at them. She closed her eyes briefly before turning her face up to study his. He saw a retort forming in her eyes and in the defiant thrust of her chin, but he saw just as visibly when she gentled her words and her anger.

"I'll wear them," she said. "I wanted to wear them. I just didn't know if I should. And now—" Her voice broke slightly. "It seems I have no choice. But I'm afraid I have no answers about them—any more than I have answers about anything else. So if you want to know more about them, I suggest you ask the woman who gave them to me this morning. I suggest you talk to your mother.

"She said this was where it all started. *What* started, Richard? I want to know. I have to know. Why won't you tell me what happened?"

*She* wanted to know? *She* had to know? "I can't tell you!" The words erupted from him full of the frustration he had felt for months. "I can't tell you," he said, "because I wasn't here. I don't know." He turned to leave. Now. Before more was said. Before *he* begged *her* for answers. Before he begged her to pretend that none of the last months had happened and that they were still back in that fantasyland where he believed the two of them might find happiness together. Mel's words of weeks ago echoed in his mind, taunting him. "I just don't know."

She owed him an apology.

Lexi woke the next morning with that thought pressing all others from her mind. Richard had come to her in the night, and she had taken his comfort and given him her anger.

Not fair. But then nothing in her life seemed fair.

Nothing in her life seemed right.

Except, somehow, Richard. And she had turned on him.

The icy rain had stopped, but now the wind whipped around the windows surrounding her bed. Lexi shivered. The light visible through the parted draperies was the gray-and-threatening light of early morning, yet Lexi knew the hour had to be late. She had rested too well for this to be a predawn hour.

Dreading the gloom, dreading the chill and dreading the oppression of this house that surely had never been a home, she threw off the covers and forced herself into the morning.

Someone, either Richard or one of the quiet, competent staff, had brought a tray containing a carafe of coffee and a basket of croissants and placed it on the table in front

of the newly freshened fire. Lexi shrugged into a robe
and poured herself a cup of steaming coffee, needing the
jolt of caffeine, before turning toward her shower and
that ridiculously opulent closet.

She couldn't find his office. She knew it was somewhere in that maze of hallways below ground level. No
one needed this much space, certainly not one woman,
one small girl and the man who had built this tribute to
wealth and power but only visited occasionally. Certainly
not the newly married couple she and Richard had
been—

*Newly married.*

Had Richard told her that?

Lexi stopped at still another closed and locked door
and slumped against it, chilled in the heavy sweater and
jeans she had been so sure would protect her in this alien
atmosphere.

For an agonizing minute the closed doors of the hallway pressed in on her. Somewhere in the depths of the
basement a pump or a motor hummed and thumped
rhythmically. That, too, pressed in on her, driving her
back until she found herself shrinking against one of
those ominous doors, while the pounding noises accel-
erated, keeping time with the ever-accelerating beat of
her heart.

"Stop it!"

She caught her hand to her mouth but couldn't stop
the whisper that followed her outcry. "Stop it," she
moaned against her fist. There was nothing here to spawn
the fear that had ambushed her.

Nothing except whatever had robbed her of her memory.

Nothing except whatever tortured her dreams and left her cringing in Richard's arms.

Nothing except whatever had brought them to this house, which both of them so obviously disliked.

Lexi drew in a shuddering breath. She wasn't trapped, she reminded herself, suddenly needing reassurance. She wasn't locked in, and she wasn't lost. She might not be able to find Richard's office, but she could find another place—a place that was warm and comforting.

Ignoring the heavy smell of chlorine from the pool, Lexi made her way to the opposite side of the conservatory to a concrete bench surrounded by a half dozen banana trees, an enormous red-flowering bougainvillea and palms that reached two or more stories high to the glass roof.

Behind her the delicate grillwork of an aviary sheltered an assortment of tropical birds, riotous in their colors and their calls. *They* were locked in. *Trapped.* And if she were foolish enough to do what her heart immediately demanded and open their cage, they would be lost.

She sank onto the bench and watched a brilliantly colored toucan preening himself.

The cage was spacious, reaching to the roof and stretching the entire width of the conservatory. Did the birds even know it was a prison?

She glanced around. Through the fronds of the palm she saw a small grouping of rattan furniture, and another chill moved through her.

Was this a prison?

Fascinated, she looked back at the gaily cushioned love seat, empty now, but...

The humid warmth of the room wasn't enough.

She had to get out of this house.

She had to leave.

Now.

A door across the room beckoned, and Lexi stood. A door to the outside. Slowly, but gaining speed as she pushed her way through the lush jungle of plants, avoiding, trying to silence the mocking whispers of the furniture, she answered the door's demand until at last she was free of the foliage and ran across the tiled verge of the pool to the door.

Locked.

She slumped against the cool glass of the door. No. Oh, no. Beyond the clear glass panes of the door, across a wide, tiled patio, freedom waited. She'd gotten this far; she couldn't stop now. She wouldn't. She scanned the edges of the door. No wires? Did that mean there was no alarm? Or only that she didn't see it? It didn't matter. She had to get out of this house. A terra-cotta turtle sat on a small ledge near the door. Lexi snatched it up, and before she had time to consider what her punishment might be this time, she pounded it against the door.

Shattered glass rained down on the tile floor as she dropped the turtle and forced the door open. Across the patio, two dark shapes rose from a sheltered corner and turned to confront her.

Dogs? There were dogs?

She stood paralyzed by fear of the massive heads and gleaming teeth facing her. Even when she heard a shout, she was unable to move, until Richard and Jack raced across a patch of lawn. She felt Richard's hands on her shoulders as he stepped between her and the dogs. She drew in a deep breath that threatened to become a moan.

*Richard's* house. *Richard's* door. She was with *Richard,* not at that other place—that other place that for one blinding moment seemed so clear yet just as quickly faded into the mists of the rest of her life. Lexi grabbed

Richard's arms, holding on to him as she tried to hold on to that illusive, terrifying memory.

"You're all right," Richard said. "You're all right, Lexi. Look at me. Look at *me*."

He took her hand, holding it between them. "You're bleeding. You've cut yourself. What were you trying to do?"

She heard a whimper and knew it had to be coming from her. The dogs heard it, too, and turned bright, watchful eyes toward her.

"Oh, God. You were trying to run away again, weren't you?"

Again?

Lexi jerked against his tightened hold on her.

Again?

"Mel!"

"I'm here, Richard. Let me see the cut."

"And will someone turn off the alarm before we have every lawman in the county up here?"

They were all there, the entire family, half the staff, both of the Handlys, watching her. Waiting. But for what? And this time she sensed that there would be no comfort from the man who held her in a ruthless grasp.

"Let's take her to my room, Richard. My bag is there."

Lexi didn't want to go to Melissa's room. Didn't want to subject herself to the cool aloofness that was Melissa Knapp. Didn't want to feel the faint, barely disguised dislike that emanated from the woman even while she was urging Lexi to share her deepest thoughts and vagrant memories. She didn't want to go anywhere but back to the delicate blue suite where even there she didn't feel safe, back to the moment last night when she had awakened to find Richard with her to chase away the fear.

To find Richard with her to share the darkness.

But she had no choice. Richard turned her and with a firm arm around her shoulders led her through the conservatory to the small, hidden elevator, and on to Melissa's room, with Melissa there with them each step of the way.

The cut was messy but not severe. While Melissa tended the wound, Richard stood silently by. Melissa nodded and stepped back, and he lifted Lexi's bandaged hand.

"I was looking for you," Lexi told him.

"And that's why you broke the door?"

"No." She had never seen him so stern, so uncompromising. Something told her she should proceed with caution, that only unpleasant things happened when she didn't, but Lexi remembered too well that other Richard, the one she had been seeking. "No. I don't know why I broke the door, only that I had to get out of that room, out of this house." She choked back a small, bitter laugh. "But that's not allowed, is it? The dogs will see to that."

Richard shook his head. "Lexi, the dogs won't—" He fell silent and studied her hand, obviously reluctant to give her a vacant promise. "No," he said, admitting what she had already suspected. "It isn't wise for you to leave the house without telling anyone, without making sure that I am with you, or Jack is, if you want to go outside."

"And I'll be allowed to?"

"Damn it, Lexi! This is our home, not a prison."

"Richard." Melissa stepped forward and placed a hand on his arm. "Leave us."

"Mel—"

"Let me do my job."

"Right." He cupped Lexi's cheek with his hand and exerted slight pressure until she looked up into his searching eyes. "Where are you, Alexandra? *Who* are you?"

Once Richard left, Lexi moved with Melissa to the alcove where she knew she would face questions she still couldn't answer. Only the room was different. In the hotel, Melissa had sat behind a graceful desk; now she sat in a matching floral boudoir chair beside Alexandra in an appearance of friendship. But Lexi knew better. Melissa Knapp was not her friend.

Lexi lay back against the chintz upholstery and closed her eyes. For weeks she had gone through this drill with Melissa, silently submitting to the woman's authority, trying to dredge up anything to appease her. Nothing had. Her silent suffering hadn't won her any points, either. Not even with herself. And no memories had come.

Only today, when she had begun exerting some unknown will, had she felt any twinges of memory. And they had been only twinges. Maybe it was time for her to question Melissa's treatment of her and its success.

She turned her head and opened her eyes, looking questioningly at the cool blond image Melissa presented to the world.

"I realize it isn't necessary for a doctor to like a patient," Lexi said, "but is it possible for you to be impartial or effective when you so actively dislike one?"

A small twitch of the right corner of Melissa's mouth acknowledged the hit. "What's not to like, Alexandra," Mel asked. "You're everything Richard ever wanted— loving, kind, *gentle*. Aren't you?"

"Am I?" It was important, now more than at any other time, to know. "If so, do I deserve the animosity I feel from everyone in this house?"

"That's what I'm attempting to find out."

What? That she was—gentle? Or that she deserved the treatment she had found here?

"Then let's do it," Lexi said. "Let's end this confusion now.... What about hypnosis? I don't trust you, Melissa, but I'd be willing to go through that, if it would help. Anything. I'm willing to do anything. You tell me. You're the doctor."

Melissa stood. "That's right. I am. And in spite of what you might think, I do have your interests at heart. So until I decide you're truly ready for any other form of treatment, we'll continue with what I've already established.

"Now, Alexandra, I want you to tell me what you were thinking when you broke the door."

# Five

By late that afternoon Lexi hadn't seen Richard again. Following the new exercise regime Melissa had imposed during their morning session, she returned to the conservatory. The door had been repaired and the remains of the glass and the turtle removed, but the smell of chlorine was just as strong. Still, the water beckoned, calling to some unknown facet of her soul. Lexi shed the terry cloth cover-up she wore over a simple black one-piece bathing suit and knelt to rake her hand through the water.

Warm. The water was warm and slid silkily, invitingly, over the suddenly sensitive flesh of her hand. Delighted, Lexi sank to the edge of the pool and swung her legs into the comforting warmth of the water. Mel had ordered her to swim. Could she? Was this something else she had lost in the darkness no one would talk about? Surely not even Mel would send her to drown.

Helene might, Lexi thought, remembering the animosity that had radiated from the older woman as Helene took the head of the table at lunch in Richard's absence, but not Mel. Mel might wish her dead, or gone, but she cared too much for the oath she had taken as a physician to violate it.

So, she probably wouldn't drown. Lexi held on to that thought as she slid into the water.

Oh, yes. Lexi surrendered to the welcoming embrace of the water around her, letting herself submerge in its depths. Heaven. Absolute heaven. Her feet found the ceramic bottom of the pool and pushed her to the surface where she dragged in air and lay back into the gentle lapping of the water against her. After a moment she turned on her side and took a tentative stroke and then another. To her delight she slid through the water with an ease and a grace she had found missing recently, in the only portion of her life she remembered.

As she broke the surface of the water, a triumphant laugh broke from her.

Which died as she saw Richard and Greg standing by the door to the adjoining gymnasium, watching her.

Greg wore a long terry cloth robe, so she suspected he had been coming to the pool. He nodded at her. "Well," he said in a voice meant to carry, meant to intimidate, "I see you haven't completely forgotten everything." Then he twisted on his crutches and retreated into the gymnasium.

Richard remained, staring at her. Across the distance of the room, Lexi suddenly felt that her joy, her exuberance in finding the water, had touched a cord within him and evoked memories of his own—memories that were far less pleasant than the sensations that had only moments ago seemed to free her from the darkness surrounding them.

She lifted her hand to push the wet hair back from her eyes. The silence in the room was broken only by the gaily bubbling fountain somewhere across the room and the chatter and calls of the birds in the aviary.

He stood there a moment longer, not speaking, before he turned and followed Greg from the room.

Lexi swam to the side of the pool and held on to it as she felt her joy fade as quickly as it had come. What on earth had that been about? Not Greg's words; she half suspected he felt that way. But Richard and that moment of silent communication that she realized should have meant something to her.

She shook her head, clearing her streaming hair from her eyes, but not clearing her thoughts. With her joy gone, her assigned exercise became just that once again, and she discovered that no matter how much she had enjoyed her swim, it had exhausted her. And she discovered that no matter how at home she had felt in the water, if it hadn't been for the abundance of ladders ringing the pool, she wasn't sure she would have known just how to get out.

Richard was not at dinner.

Helene once again claimed the chair at the head of the table, this time in the massive, oppressive dining room. The four of them seemed lost at the huge table, almost as lost as the young woman who served the meal.

"I suppose he's off on another book tour," Helene said. "You might know that the moment he could, he'd abandon all his responsibilities to his family."

Lexi glanced up sharply.

Mel stared at the woman with barely controlled dislike. "I don't see devoting the past eight months of his life to this family as abandoning responsibility."

"No, but then you're hardly an impartial observer of anything that pertains to my oldest son, are you Melissa?"

Greg threw his napkin on the table and struggled up and out of the heavy chair. "For God's sake, Mother, why not just announce to the world that my wife is in love with my brother?"

"No!"

The cry came from Melissa, but it might well have been Lexi's. She turned to look at the woman, but Mel's eyes were focused on Greg.

"No," Mel repeated more softly. "You can't believe that."

"Why not?" Greg stumbled as he fitted his twisted hands into his crutches. He nodded derisively toward Lexi. "What man wouldn't prefer you, dear wife, to a thief and a liar like her, to someone who couldn't stick around long enough to find out if he was alive or dead?" His mouth twisted. "And what woman wouldn't prefer him, even as scarred as he is, to the wreck I've become?"

Lexi cried that night. Alone in the silk-curtained corner of her room, alone in the huge bed that was meant to be shared, she felt tears streaming silently down her face, cold on her cheeks in the dark of the night.

It wasn't something she would have called out to Richard to help her through, even if he had been there. At least she didn't think it was. But it didn't matter. For the first time in her limited memory, Richard was not near.

*A thief and a liar.* Could it be true? And could she have abandoned him?

That would explain so much.

But not the ominous fleeting glimpses of the past she had felt since returning to this house.

And not the gentleness he had shown her every night when she awoke terrified of some unknown menace.

But it would explain the distance he kept from her except at those times; it would explain the animosity Mel, Greg, Helene and even Mrs. Handly showed her. It would explain so much, but it seemed so wrong.

She swiped at her tears, hating the weakness that made them possible, hating the darkness that hid the cause of them from her. She had left the door between her room and Richard's open, as he had insisted, but she heard no sound from the other room, saw no light, felt no energy, telling her that he had at last returned from whatever had taken him from the house.

Lexi gathered her robe around her and walked to the connecting door. Richard's room lay in darkness, except for the bright moonlight spilling through the wall of windows onto the empty bed. She looked at the windows and the bed, feeling a fleeting tug of déjà vu. She willed herself to be still, to let what would surface, surface, because she had learned that fighting for memory only forced it away, but nothing came.

She choked back a bitter laugh and returned to the warmth of her bed. Nothing ever came. The thwarted laugh became a moan. Was she destined to spend the rest of her life not knowing what had happened to bring her to this point? Was she destined to spend the rest of her life surrounded by people who barely tolerated her and not know *why?*

A thief and a liar?

Was she?

Was that why Richard wouldn't tell her what had happened? He wouldn't stay married to her if that were true, would he? He would cast her away and she'd be alone, with no one. Without a past, without a future. Without him.

*Where was he tonight?*

But that was none of her business, was it?

She turned in the bed, feeling a pang of loneliness, of despair, that threatened to overpower her fragile defenses. She wouldn't give in to it. She couldn't. She hugged her pillow close and prayed for the peace of sleep.

*A dark, lean form stood before a narrow, uncurtained window with his back to her. But even in the dim light, she saw the tension that held him immobile. Her angel. Her beautiful dark angel. And now he needed her.*

*She walked to him, feeling curiously weightless in what even in her enchantment she recognized as a dream. Unafraid, she circled his waist with her arms. "Why?" she asked, resting her head against his bare back. "Why?"*

*He covered her hands with his, holding them tightly against him, as he breathed deeply and harshly. "Get away from me, Alexandra," he said, even as he held her hands imprisoned. "Get away before I hurt you more than you've already been hurt."*

*She felt a moment of instant, involuntary hesitation, then banished it. This was what she wanted, had wanted for weeks. She surrendered to the unaccustomed intimacy and molded herself to him, feeling through her simple cotton shift the muscles and ribs of his back against her throbbing breasts, and his need, the strength and the vulnerability of him beneath her touch.*

*"You aren't running from me." She felt his words as they were torn from him.*

*"I won't," she said, and slanted her head to place a series of tiny kisses across his shoulder but wanting to give him more, much more. "Not ever."*

*"Alexandra."* *He groaned and turned, crushing her against him. She went up on her tiptoes, circling his neck with her arms, but even that wasn't enough, and he lifted her. He covered her mouth with his with bruising hunger that echoed the wildness of the heated blood now coursing through her. She whimpered when he tore his mouth from hers and released his grasp so that she slid down the length of him until her feet once again touched the floor.*

*"I want you," he said, but she heard all the softer words he would not let himself say. I love you. I need you.*

*His eyes were as dark as the night outside and held as many secrets. This was the moment, she knew. If she had any doubts, this was the moment to pull away. He would let her. She closed her heart to her doubts. If she rejected him now, he would close himself off again.*

*She felt the tension cording the muscles in his neck beneath her hands and moved her fingers upward, soothing and yet demanding something she barely understood. She lifted one hand and traced it across his jaw, finding the strength of it hidden beneath the wild growth of beard that had served to disguise him. Gently, persistently with her hands, she demanded that he bend toward her. "And I want you."*

*He remained still and unyielding, but she felt the energy coiled within him.*

*"I don't want to hurt you," he said. "I—I haven't been with a woman in—"*

*She slid her hand from his cheek to his lips, silencing him. "And I..." She hesitated. It was a little lie, one that he would forgive her for later, perhaps. "It's been a while for me, too."*

*She felt his lips moving beneath her fingers as he*

turned his face to meet the caress of her hand and then his gentle probing of her palm.

She loved this man. Even if he would never believe her, while he held her she could show him how much she loved him. She raised herself on her toes again and freed her hand from his mouth to slide it around his neck. This time the demand that he bend toward her was more insistent. Oh, yes, she could show him.

When he covered her mouth with his, his hunger was still there, but now it was leashed. When he lifted her, it was to move with her, to carry her to the rumpled narrow bed and lay her on it. Dropping down beside her, he never once broke the life-sustaining contact of mouth, lips, tongue.

Without the need to support her, his hands were free to move over her. He used that freedom. It was as though he had to sense each part of her, to brand each part of her as his. But her hands were free, too, and her need to know him as great as his to know her.

When he lifted her to remove the last of her clothing, she felt her hair spilling over his arm, whispering silkily across the flesh of her back, and then all thoughts of her hair were forgotten, because his flesh, firm, hair-roughened and heated, met hers.

The weight of him, the feel of him beneath her hands and mouth, the scent of him, clean from the showers they had finally been able to take, heady and masculine, the moist probing of his tongue and barely restrained savagery of his lips in intimacies she had scarcely imagined before only fed her own urgency—an urgency she had not thought possible. She moved beneath him, intuition guiding her hands and her mouth. His ragged intake of breath and the quivering of his muscles confirmed the *accuracy of that intuition, until she felt him nudging her, seeking entrance.*

*She opened her eyes and looked up. The muscles of his arms and shoulders corded and strained as he supported his weight on them. Looking into the midnight depths of his eyes, she knew that in this she must show no hesitancy. She lifted her hands to his back and then slid them lower to urge him to her, to complete what she had known to be necessary since the moment he had torn her from her hiding place.*

*"No!" the word ripped from him when he met the unexpected barrier.*

*"Yes," she whispered. "Oh, yes." Lifting her hips, she pushed him past the moment of restraint, and he surged into her.*

*His! His in a way she had longed for but believed could never happen. She lay still, adjusting to his possession, watching the changing expressions on his face. A shadow darkened his features. Regret? Please, oh, please, she thought, don't let it be regret. Then he was moving within her, hard driving thrusts careening rapidly out of control, thrusts that fired her blood, fired the already-molten center of her. She was moving with him, toward still another place of safety, but this time, with him, in a truth and a beauty and a love that not even he would be able to deny.*

*Later, when speech was once again possible, while he held her close as though he thought she might try to escape, he smoothed a tendril of damp hair from her cheek and pulled her head onto his chest.*

*"Why didn't you tell me?" he asked.*

*"It isn't expected at my age," she said. "I didn't want to stop to explain. I—I didn't want to stop...you." She twisted her head, but she couldn't see his face.*

*"I don't think I could have stopped," he admitted.*

*"I've wanted you too long. But you deserved more. I could have been more gentle with you."*

She remembered the passion he had finally unleashed and doubted his words. He was a man who had been too long without love. She bit gently at the flesh of his chest and caressed the nip with her tongue. *"Could you have been?"*

He exhaled slowly. *"I don't know."* He turned and covered her with his weight. *"Not the first time. But now—now I think I might be able to."*

And he was. Oh, yes, he was. Each touch showed her how much he treasured her, and later still as she lay in his arms, drained of all desire to think coherently or to speak, his words reflected the love he had shown her but still not spoken.

*"You aren't protected are you?"* he asked.

She shook her head against his chest.

*"Don't worry,"* he promised her, folding himself more closely around her. *"After tonight, I'll take care of you."*

"Lexi. Lexi, wake up."

She lifted her fingers to his face, to his smooth, shaven cheek.

"You've lost your beard," she said in wonder, feeling a subtle shift in the quality of his touch.

"Wake up," he said again, holding firmly to her shoulders and setting her away from the warmth of his embrace.

She reached for him and felt the texture of finely woven wool beneath her hands.

"Richard?"

He sighed and released her. "Yes. You were dreaming again."

He sat on the edge of her bed, fully dressed, in an

expertly tailored business suit and crisp shirt. "Tell me what you remember."

Lexi released one long quavering breath. A dream. Oh, yes. Far different from those that usually haunted her sleep, but a dream just the same. Hadn't she at some level known that? She glanced at Richard's familiar features and found herself trapped in memories. Had she really known him as well as the fragments of thoughts that remained with her told her she had? Had he really felt the way she had thought? The heat of a blush rushed through her. Had she really felt free enough to do those things with this man?

"Tell me," he said again.

*Oh, no.* There was no way she could admit to him the pleasure she had felt in his arms. She felt a chill steal the lingering warmth of nighttime memories. There was no way she could tell him that even in her dream, even at the most intimate of moments, she had knowingly, willingly, lied to him. So she did the only thing she knew to do. She moved the few inches necessary to completely separate them, looked at him across the darkness and knew that she would have to lie again, at least for the moment. "I don't remember."

Richard met her for breakfast. Dressed again in a black long-sleeved turtleneck sweater and casual slacks, he knocked on the connecting door and stepped into her room just as she emerged, wearing jeans and a sweater, from her dressing room.

"I thought we'd go down together this morning," he said. "I understand that dinner was not a pleasant experience."

He spoke as though nothing had happened the night before. Lexi hesitated, until she found that she was rubbing distractedly at the antique rings on her finger, until she realized that for him nothing had happened.

He said nothing about where he had been for most of the evening; he said nothing about why he had broken what was apparently a strict at-home schedule by being with her instead of locked in his office. And of course it would do her no good to ask for answers. The past weeks had taught her that.

"No," she admitted. "No, it wasn't."

"Lexi, are you all right?"

But he could, and did, ask for answers to her each and every thought and word and expression. She released her grip on the rings and lifted her chin. He stepped closer and lifted his hand to her cheek, touching her briefly before stepping back, and for a moment, only a moment, a tentative smile lit his eyes. "I know," he said, repeating her own words of the night they arrived at this monstrous house, "'Foolish question.'"

Mrs. Handly met them in the breakfast room, setting out two beautifully prepared plates as Richard escorted Lexi into the room, and Lexi saw thankfully that no other places were set at the table. She didn't think she had the strength for another family meal, not quite yet…maybe never. Richard seated her, and Lexi looked at her breakfast—tropical fruit, melon, a delicate roll of some sort—and sighed in appreciation.

"Thank you," she said, looking up at the housekeeper. "It's been so long since I—"

*Since I what?*

In her shock, Lexi almost missed the questioning glance Eva Handly gave Richard. Almost.

"Yes, thank you, Eva," Richard said, filling the awkward silence and freeing the housekeeper to make her exit.

Lexi lifted her napkin from beside her plate and twisted it in her hands. "Don't ask me to finish that statement," she said. "Don't ask me where it came from. Don't ask me what it meant."

She felt the glitter of unshed tears in her eyes. "But you don't have to ask, do you? You already know the answers."

"Some of them, Alexandra," he admitted. "Only some of them. But every day I discover there are more I need to learn."

He seated himself beside her. "Eat," he said. "I think this morning is warm enough for us to take that outside tour I promised you."

As the morning wore on, Lexi knew something had changed in Richard's attitude toward her. True, the difference in his actions was subtle, but it was there. The dogs accompanied them, running up, alert and eager the moment they stepped from the service entrance, but falling back a distance at Richard's command. Lexi walked beside him, bundled now against the ever-present chill sweeping in from the lake, and knowing he slowed and shortened his stride for her benefit as he led her through the tangle of formal gardens toward the stone wall that bordered the property. On the other side of the wall, the forest of oak and scrubby, stunted trees encroached. They followed the wall to the point where it disappeared into the waters of the lake and then followed the rock-strewn shoreline.

Different. So different. And yet somehow familiar. The wind stilled for a moment, and Lexi stepped closer to the water. A strangely delicate rock captured her attention, and she picked it up. She heard a childish giggle and saw herself lifting a shell in one hand as she stood barefooted in warm sand near clear blue water.

*"¿Quanto?"* she heard herself ask.

*"Uno."* The answer came from a dark-haired imp no more than five, with huge dark eyes, who stood in the middle of a cluster of children his age.

"No, no," she again heard herself say over the laugh that threatened to break free and embarrass the child. *"En Ingles, por favor."*

The boy swaggered forward and cast a disparaging glance over his shoulder at the giggling children. "One," he said. "One, Teacher. One, two, three."

A chill wind swept over the lake, clearing away this tiny fragment of another life. She clenched her hand over the rock but knew there would be no more...no more. Her shoulders slumped and she turned to find Richard studying her. He'd ask; she might as well answer, but with a question of her own. "Where—where's the child?"

He blanched. His unhealthy pallor became if possible even more gray; his dark eyes, stark. "Which...which child?"

*Damn him!* Damn Mel and her rules and strictures. Damn the darkness that hid even the simplest knowledge from her. "The child I taught," she said evenly, determined to reveal none of her frustration and knowing she lost that battle. "No...no. The *children.* The ones to whom I spoke Spanish. I speak Spanish, don't I, Richard?" She tested the language and found it waiting. *"¿Hablo espanol?"*

He turned from her, looking out over the lake. "Yes," he told her. "And French, a little Greek and a couple of Indian dialects."

A linguist and a teacher, at least of sorts. "Then I'm not quite the idiot everyone treats me as?"

"No one ever said you were an idiot, Lexi."

"No?" She heard her voice rise and struggled to control it. "Simple-minded then. Incapable of making even the smallest decision in my recovery or in anything else. *Perdida,* Richard, if that's not treating me like an idiot, what would you call it?"

"Caring for you," he said quietly. "Wanting what's best for you, even if we don't quite know what it is. Surely you don't fault us for that."

Fault *us?* Lexi heard other words in that question. *Fault me?* he asked.

The anger went out of her, leaving only a bleak despair. "No, Richard," she said. "I don't fault you. I know that you—you are doing the best you know. I know that without you the past weeks would have been unbearable." Could she admit this? He knew so much about her and she so little. But he had never ceased to comfort her in the night when the demons prowled. And he had never thrown those demons at her in the harsh light of morning.

"I'm afraid," she admitted. "That I won't ever find out what happened in my past. That I will and won't be able to stand that knowledge. Who am I, Richard?" she asked. "What did I do to bring me to this point?"

He stepped closer to her, almost as though he had to do so. For a moment he only looked down at her and then, slowly, cautiously, his arms went around her, bringing her against the warmth and security of his chest, against the safety of him, the strength of him.

She looked up at him and he lifted his hands to her face as he met her exploration with one of his own before his eyes darkened, his head bent, and as though this, too, he had to do, he lowered his mouth to hers.

*I know this touch.*

From countless nights, she knew it. From countless

longings, she knew it. From more, much more, still hidden from her, she knew it. She sighed and surrendered to the welcome and never-hoped-for sense of homecoming that washed through her. *Oh, Richard, Richard, my darling, I've missed you.*

Too soon she felt him drawing away from her, heard his ragged breath that told her he had not been unaffected, felt the strength of his hands on her shoulders as he began physically moving back from her and her needy touch.

"We can't do this," he said unevenly.

Bereft. Alone. The chill wind sliced through her. "Why?" she asked. "Why?"

"Because you don't know me, Alexandra. And because, God help me, I don't know you."

# Six

Lexi searched her room again, methodically, at first, in the minutes after Richard escorted her there and left her alone, and then, when she continued to find nothing, with a sense of desperation. Somewhere, somehow, she had to find a clue to the person she was—to the person she had been.

She had searched before, Richard had searched, and even Helene had searched these rooms. Which one of them had removed all traces of her past?

Only the room itself, so different from the oppression of the rest of the house, and the contents of her closet, if she had in fact chosen them, gave her any hint of the woman who had occupied these rooms.

And nothing remained hidden. All drawers opened to her touch, all cabinets, all doors except the one in her dressing room that led to the unrenovated sunroom that Richard had told her was unsafe to explore.

The wind whirled around the house, forcing its way through the narrow opening framed by grillwork above the locked door, and rattled the panes in the windows surrounding her bed. Following quickly came the pelting of rain, drowning out the sounds of the angry lashing of the lake against the rock-strewn shore.

There were no books in this room, no photographs, no receipts or hurriedly scrawled notes tucked away and forgotten in a drawer or a pocket. Nothing. Lexi shivered and shrugged into an oversize cardigan, although her chill wasn't entirely caused by the dropping temperatures. It was as though she hadn't existed before she'd awakened in that Boston hotel room—or as though someone wished she hadn't and had erased every sign of her existence.

Richard would tell her nothing more; Mel would tell her nothing at all. Surely someone in the faded mausoleum of a house could tell her—*would* tell her—something.

Mrs. Handly. *We've worked for Mr. Jordan for years, here—and for you.*

The route down the back stairs would be quicker and more private. Lexi stopped at the top of them, telling herself to go on, but there was no way she could force herself into that narrow hallway. Was this another memory resting just below the surface of her consciousness? She knew she would have to examine her reasons sometime. But not now. Not now.

Trembling, telling herself there was no reason to, she backed away from the doorway and turned toward the front stairs. The door to Mel's room opened just as Lexi reached the main hallway.

Hesitating, not wanting to see the woman until she could no longer avoid the daily session, Lexi paused, half hidden by an enormous armoire. But it wasn't Mel who came out of the room; it was Richard. Lexi grasped the armoire for support. There were any number of reasons he would have been in Mel's room—Lexi knew that, and told herself that. Any number of valid, innocent reasons.

He didn't look her way, but she glimpsed the scowl that darkened his features as he looked back into Mel's suite.

"I don't care what your sources say, Melissa. The woman I knew wouldn't have—*couldn't* have done that. Anything else, but not...not that."

Melissa appeared in the doorway and placed her slender, beautifully manicured hand on Richard's arm. "I know what you must be thinking, Richard, what you must be feeling."

"Do you?" he asked in a voice that was little more than a groan. "Can you?"

Lexi didn't know who reached for whom, but as she watched, Richard and Melissa caught each other in an embrace. The diamond in Melissa's wedding ring glittered obscenely against the dark sweater covering Richard's shoulders. Lexi caught her hand to her mouth to hold back a moan as she witnessed this intense scene. Soon, though, with his hands on her shoulders, Richard held Melissa away from him.

"Don't let what you want to see blind you," Melissa said as she lifted her hand to trace delicately along the abrasions still marring his cheek. "You're trained in finding the truth, no matter how ugly or painful it is."

Richard looked into Mel's eyes for what seemed an eternity before taking the one step back that separated them. "Yes," he said. "Yes, I am. And that is exactly what I am trying to do."

Then he left, striding down the hall toward his room,

and Melissa stepped back into her room and closed the door.

Lexi sagged against the armoire. What she had just witnessed had been intimate and passionate. But had it been the intimacy and passion of lovers, as Greg insisted, or something different—something that didn't betray the vows that each of them had taken?

And she—was she the woman they were talking about? What had she done? And how had Richard been trained to learn the truth? Through the writing she'd heard veiled references to?

Whatever she had witnessed, Lexi knew she couldn't remain where she was, just waiting to be discovered and questioned. But as she didn't want to be questioned, she found that she no longer had the strength or desire to question anyone else.

The memory of the library downstairs teased her into moving. A deep leather chair, a soothing fire and a book to escape into seemed the perfect answer as to how to spend the rest of this ruined morning. If she were lucky, she could read through lunch and not have to see or think about anyone who lived in this house until dinnertime— not even... Not even Richard. Richard. He was the one person she most wanted to see. But she knew that she didn't dare, because if she once began questioning him, she might never be able to stop. Right now, she wasn't sure she could live with any of the answers he might give.

Peace was not to be hers. Someone else had claimed the library. Lexi paused outside the partially opened door as the sound of voices drifted to her.

No.

She would not eavesdrop again, especially not on Helene.

Let Helene berate whoever she wanted; Lexi didn't want any part of someone else's feud. She didn't know these people; she didn't know the intricacies of their relationships or the emotional baggage that prompted their actions.

She took a step away from the door. It wasn't her fight. *It wasn't.* But no one deserved the derision she heard in Helene's relentless voice. No one deserved the condescension or the utter lack of respect.

It wasn't her fight, she repeated to herself. But she stepped forward and pushed open the door.

No one in the house was her friend, but Eva Handly, the woman being subjected to Helene's diatribe, had at least not been openly hostile. Eva glanced up, and, seeing Lexi in the doorway behind Helene, attempted some sort of signal with her eyes. What? To go away? To leave her to endure this alone?

"You will do as I say," Helene continued, apparently unaware of Lexi's presence. "You will do *exactly* as I say in matters of running this house. That includes serving meals when and where I want. You...not some inexperienced girl with no proper sense of protocol, or you will be dismissed. You and your husband. Again. And this time there will be a reference...a negative one that will follow you wherever you attempt to go. Have I made myself clear?"

She didn't want to do this. Under no circumstances did she want to be embroiled in a fight with Richard's mother, not even with the ambivalent feelings Richard himself felt about the woman who had given him birth. But having witnessed this injustice, Lexi knew she couldn't walk away from it.

"How very interesting," she said, praying her voice wouldn't betray the fear she felt as she stumbled into this fray. "But I believe this is Richard's house and therefore any decisions concerning it are his to make."

She saw Helene's shoulders stiffen before the woman turned to face her. "Alexandra. Why don't you go back upstairs, dear? We're all aware of your fragile condition, and, really, this is no business of yours."

Exactly! Helene's words echoed Lexi's sentiments, but seeing the moment of unmasked hatred in the older woman's eyes and hearing her speak as though Lexi were a not-too-bright child only strengthened her resolve to defend Mrs. H.

"Oh. Foolish me. I thought because everyone tells me I am Richard's wife that the running of our household and the employment of staff would be my business."

Helene's mouth tightened, but before she could speak, Lexi shrugged. "In any event, it *is* Richard's business." It was, and since Lexi had seen how easily he interacted with Eva, she suspected he would not be any happier about this mistreatment of the woman than she was. "I just saw him go into his room. Shall we call him to arbitrate?"

"What a hypocritical child you have become!" Helene fairly snapped the words at her. "And of course you have forgotten that you, yourself, threw these people out on the street without so much as a moment's notice.

"Oh, never mind." Helene turned back toward the housekeeper. "I will not tolerate insubordination or rudeness. Do you understand? One more episode and I *will* take this to my son."

"Yes, Mrs. Knapp. I understand completely."

The strength in Lexi's knees lasted only until Helene had stalked from the room. She sank gratefully into the nearest wing chair and fought against the tremor that worked through her. Eva remained standing in the same spot and the same position as when Lexi entered the room, but now her gray eyes studied Lexi intently. Apparently reaching a decision, she stepped toward Lexi and extended her hand to help her from the chair.

"Come with me." It was an invitation and a command.

Lexi nodded and fell into step beside the woman, who led her toward the back of the house.

"You were a quiet little thing when Richard brought you here," Mrs. Handly said as they reached the kitchen. "Until you thought someone was being mistreated. Then you came out with all claws extended." She paused beside a cabinet with a huge wooden breadboard surface. "It was impressive—more like a kitten than a mountain lion." A hint of a smile briefly softened the woman's face. "But your heart was good, and so were your intentions.

"That's why we were so...so shocked at the change."

An answer. An honest answer to a question she hadn't asked. Lexi gripped the edge of the cabinet. "I fired you?" she asked. "Why?"

"We never knew." Eva began gathering supplies and placing them on the countertop: bowls, measurers, yeast. "We never knew. Melissa came for Richard, and went with him. At least as far as he would let her go. You got sick right after they left. We thought it was probably only a virus of some sort. Then you sent word you didn't want me bringing your meals to you, or Jack tending the fireplace in your room. You cut yourself off from everyone but Mrs. Knapp—Helene, who had shown up unexpectedly and uninvited to wait for Greg's rescue," Mrs. Handly said, answering another question before Lexi could ask it.

"Then one night, only a day or two after Richard was

reported missing, you stood on the landing of the front stairs—didn't even come all the way down—and ordered us to leave. That night. Said you'd have our things packed and sent to us. And you did.''

Lexi saw the hurt in the woman's eyes and heard it in her voice. ''Mrs. H.?'' Yes. Yes that sounded right. ''I called you that, didn't I?''

Eva Handly sighed and jerked her head in a quick nod. ''Yes. When it was just the two of us.''

''I'm sorry I hurt you.''

Eva nodded again. ''And Richard. He didn't speak of it, but I saw the pain your leaving caused him. If I hadn't known you before, if I hadn't wondered countless times what pain you yourself had gone through to change you the way you changed, I wouldn't be speaking to you now.''

Oh, dear Lord. In her innocent way, Mrs. Handly had opened all sorts of images in Lexi's mind, all sorts of paths she didn't want to explore but knew she must. Mel was wrong to deny her this information. So wrong. ''Missing. Richard was missing? Where did he and Melissa go? Why? And why didn't I go with them?''

She saw the woman visibly withdraw. She still stood there, only a few feet away, but the time for confidence had passed.

''Please,'' Lexi said.

Mrs. Handly opened a cabinet door and exposed a huge bin of flour. Lexi heard the door closing on Mrs. H.'s previous confidence and suppressed a sigh. No, she wasn't going to answer.

''This is something else you did. You said it helped you to think, to put all things in perspective, and in some instances to vent a little frustration.''

Another unexpected gift? Another glimpse of her past?
"I baked?"

"You told me that the nuns who taught you insisted
that you learn this, too."

"I baked." It wasn't enough. Not with all the questions she now had clamoring through her. But it helped.
Yes. It helped. Yes. She felt her hands begin a suddenly
remembered kneading rhythm. Oh, yes, she had done this
often. And well.

"You insisted all your meals be served in the breakfast
room, except when you were alone. Then you took them
here, most often helping prepare them. You were redecorating this house, slowly and systematically getting rid
of the gloom that envelops it and turning it into a home.
And you hated the dining room," Eva said, returning at
last to the lecture Lexi had disrupted in the library. "You
refused to use it and had it next on your list to redeco-
rate."

Even though Mrs. H. had refused to explain so much,
Lexi had just been given a priceless gift: truth, honesty
and a piece of her lost soul. She blinked back grateful
tears. "Thank you."

Mrs. H. nodded again. She didn't smile, but her expression was somehow softer, more accepting than Lexi
remembered seeing. She handed Lexi the flour scoop.
"Here," she said. "It seems to me that this is a very
good time for you to think, to put things in perspective,
and maybe to vent a little frustration. Your French bread
is good, but if you're really frustrated, you might consider making a batch of your croissants."

Lexi was thoroughly engrossed in the dough, discov-
ering, or rediscovering how satisfying kneading, thump-
ing, taking out her frustrations on, or just getting lost in

the rhythm of working the dough was. At some point
Eva had tied an apron over Lexi's clothes and left her
alone with the therapy of the bread.

"Eva? I'll be gone several hours. I don't know—"

Richard came through the swinging door from the pan-
try and stopped just inside the kitchen as Lexi whirled
around. "Alexandra?"

He'd dressed in another of those sinfully attractive
well-tailored dark suits and carried a dark wool overcoat.
Lexi felt her heart literally stop and then begin pounding
like the wildest surf.

"You're...baking?"

She was neat when she worked, Lexi had already discovered, almost compulsively tidy. She picked up a white
cotton cloth and wiped at her hands. Whether this was
part of her compulsion or an attempt to keep from reaching for Richard, to straighten his already-straight tie or
to caress the slight abrasion of his jaw, Lexi did not
know.

"Yes," she said, gesturing toward two already-shaped
and rising loaves at the edge of the counter, and then
wondered if somehow she had broken some unspoken
taboo. Would the wife of the man who owned this monstrous house busy herself with something as homey as
making bread? "It's—it's all right, isn't it?"

A nerve twitched in Richard's scarred cheek. From anger? From frustration? She didn't know and he didn't say.
"You...remember?"

And of course, it all came back to that.

She turned toward the counter and carefully, meticu-
lously, placed the towel over the dough she had been
kneading. "No," she said, studying the array of ingre-
dients and equipment so neatly arranged in her work-

space. "My heart does, and apparently my hands do. But my mind has no conscious memory of what I'm doing."

Just as right now, her heart knew that she had known this man, had loved him, had lain with him, and her hands ached to touch him again as they must have in the past. But her conscious memories lay locked in some dark, hidden vault.

"Mrs. Handly told me. She told me I had learned from 'the nuns.' Don't worry, though. That didn't start a flood of memories." Lexi blinked back unwanted moisture in her eyes and bid a reluctant goodbye to the peace that had filled the last hour. With one last, ineffectual pat to the cloth-covered dough, she turned toward Richard. He had moved closer. Much closer.

"I don't know where Mrs. H. went," she told him even as she felt herself shrinking against the counter. "She was who you were looking for, wasn't she?"

"So restrained," Richard said, almost to himself. "So damned—timid. Where have you—"

"Richard?" she asked.

His head jerked up, and the nerve in his cheek twitched again, and she knew that she was not brave enough at this moment to broach the subjects Eva had raised.

"Yes. Yes," he said. "I'm going to be away for several hours. I want her to know I won't be here for dinner."

"Lucky you." The words popped out before she even knew she felt them and hung between them in the silence of the room.

She thought for a moment he would touch her; she hoped for a moment that he would. Instead, he shifted the overcoat from one arm to the other. "Meals haven't been pleasant for you, have they?"

She felt a glimmer of a smile play across her mouth.

This question was on a par with an earlier one of his, when he had asked her if she were all right. "That's probably a fair statement," she said, searching for a lightness she was far from feeling.

"I have appointments to keep, meetings already set up. I'm sorry, but I can't take you with me today."

She hadn't thought there was a hope of that. Obviously her expression told him that. Now he grimaced. He lifted his hand, but instead of reaching for her, he ran it distractedly over his forehead. "Lexi, I—"

He studied her carefully for long seconds. Finally he nodded. "There are events neither of us understands at work here, Alexandra, but for now there are some undeniable facts. You are my wife. This is your home. Those other people are your guests."

"You make it sound so simple."

"Believe me. Nothing in our lives is simple right now. But you don't have to take an emotional beating from anyone, especially from anyone imposing on my—on our hospitality."

But what if *she* were the one imposing. "Richard?"

No. She wouldn't risk asking that. Not until she was more sure that she wasn't. But if she were to do what his words seemed to say she could do, would there be repercussions?

"Your mother told me I fired the Handlys."

He didn't answer her with words, but he didn't have to. She saw the truth in his expression. *Why?* Why had she dismissed someone who so obviously had been her ally?

"You won't let me do that again, will you?"

"No. No, Alexandra. I won't."

"Good." She saw obvious relief in his eyes, which

made the next question easier to ask. "And you won't let anyone else do so, will you?"

He didn't ask who that anyone else might be. Nor did he pause to consider his answer. "No. I won't."

He might have said more; Lexi sensed that he wanted to, but at that moment the door behind him swung open, and Mrs. Handly returned to the kitchen. She glanced at the two of them standing in awkward silence and turned to leave.

"Wait, Eva," Richard said. "I was looking for you." With a last glance at Lexi, he walked to the house-keeper's side. "Come with me," he said. "I'm on my way out, but there are a few things I need to discuss with you."

The two of them left in silence, and Lexi sagged back against the cabinet, her peace fully shattered, and her mind racing with unanswered questions.

*You are my wife,* Richard had said. *This is your home.*

Since the morning she woke up in the Boston hotel room with Richard keeping vigil over her, she had felt like a poor relation or an unwanted dependent. Could it be? Did he really expect her to act as though this was her home? That she had the right to make decisions about it?

*Those other people are your guests.*

That was certainly what he had said.

*You are my wife.*

He had said that, too.

In spite of what Eva had let slip.

The gates swung open with a touch of the remote he carried. Richard drove through and waited until they closed behind him, locking the world out, or, as he had thought too many times, locking him in.

He hated the house and all it stood for. How ironic that twice now he had sought refuge here.

Scattered lights from the house told him that at least someone was awake, but Alexandra's room was on the lake side, not visible from the drive.

Maybe he should have taken her with him today and ended, at last, the confusion surrounding her disappearance. Telling her who his appointments were with, and why, might have been more merciful than leaving her alone to face Helene's pitiful, twisted obsession with this pile of rocks and lumber.

But he hadn't taken her. As much as he wanted to believe her incapable of the betrayal every clue he had followed until today screamed that she had committed, the words of her message, delivered by Helene as he lay near death, *Now his body is as scarred as his soul,* haunted him.

He'd had no choice but to let Alexandra go. He hadn't fought the divorce she'd begun, hadn't searched for her to reclaim the missing money. He'd done nothing, in fact, except fight the injuries to his body caused by the crash and the nearly fatal wound to his soul caused by her leaving—a wound that would have been fatal had he been told about the child.

He drove into the waiting garage. Two dark shapes emerged from the shrubbery as he stepped from his car. Richard spoke softly and the dogs went on their way, patrolling the grounds.

There was at least one lie in Lexi's medical records. He had proof of that. Melissa Knapp had not been the admitting doctor; she had been at her husband's bedside in a hospital half the world away at that time. And if there was one, were there more? Yes. Yes. If what he'd found today held even a grain of truth, there were many more.

*You're trained in finding the truth, no matter how ugly or painful it is.* Why had it taken so long for him to remember that?

*Don't let what you want to see blind you.* Was that what he was doing? Or was that what he had done from the first?

And if the records were lies, all lies, how had Alexandra come to be in Hampton's hospital? Who had been close enough to plan this grotesque deception? Who had been close enough to take the photograph he had found in Lexi's shoe and close enough to make sure she received it?

Entering the house, he was greeted by Eva Handly before heading upstairs. But Lexi wasn't in her room.

Richard hadn't known what to expect, but it wasn't to find an empty room.

Although it was after midnight, her bed was still neatly made. The remnants of a fire glowed in the fireplace, but the grouping of furniture surrounding it seemed as untouched as the bed. The door to her dressing room was closed. Thinking she must be preparing for bed, Richard stole a few minutes to shed his business suit, to ease into clothing that would seem less formidable, less confrontational—she'd apparently had enough of that for the night. But when he walked back into her room, she still hadn't returned, and he heard no sounds from the dressing room.

Tentatively he knocked on that door. "Lexi?"

He heard no answer. No sound. He tried the door, and it opened to him, showing him only shadows. He glanced sharply at the door across the room, but it remained tightly closed.

*Gone.*

Again.

Richard grabbed the door facing to keep from running from the room. Gone? At this time of night?

How?

No. No. That couldn't be right. Only minutes ago Eva had told him she'd seen Lexi about ten that night when she came to check on her, that she had been tense and strained following another disastrous meal but she was trying to hide it.

The dogs were free on the grounds. The house alarms had been set hours ago. Jack and Eva were still awake. They'd have heard any disturbance, any indication that someone—that *Lexi*—had tried to leave.

Richard turned. The small teapot Eva told him she'd brought sat on the coffee table in front of the fireplace. One almost-empty cup sat beside it. He crossed to the table and lifted the delicate china pot. It was empty. Lexi had been here, in this room, long enough to drink the tea.

He returned the pot to the tray and slumped down onto the sofa. He noticed the fine tremor in his hands and clasped them tightly together. He'd faced death with less emotion than he felt thinking that his wife had once again left him. God!

And why was he so quick to think this?

Because he'd failed her?

Again?

Because if he was too quick to think this now, had he been too quick to believe it months ago?

But where was she?

Once he had thought he knew her well enough to know where she would have gone in the middle of the night, tense, upset and strained by emotions and intrigues she had no way of understanding. Once he'd thought she would have come to him.

But he hadn't been here for her.

And he didn't know this quiet shadow of the woman who had stolen his heart and then, he'd believed, destroyed it.

Or did he?

She was remembering. Not much. And not in any pattern that he could discern.

But if she was remembering, would she remember the one place in this monstrous tribute to a man's vanity that she had truly felt at home?

In the conservatory, the lights from the pool cast watery, otherworldly shadows among the towering palms. Richard found Lexi seated on a curved concrete bench near the gate to the aviary. She looked up as he approached her, but she didn't speak and she didn't move.

Tense, yes. Strained, yes. Trying to hide it? Maybe no longer.

The rattan furniture grouping was within sight, even in the shadowy darkness. Once, a lifetime ago, she had delightedly selected that furniture grouping, but tonight she had chosen not to sit there. Memories? And if so, of what?

Of laughing with him as he peeled them both from their wet bathing suits and made love to her on the gaily patterned chaise that now waited empty, silent and dark, only a few feet away? Or of the photo that he had taken from her hands after she again lost consciousness that first night in the hotel? The photo he had locked safely away but could never forget?

*Who?* he asked himself again. Who had been close enough to take that photo? He'd rehired the Handlys as soon as he returned. He'd rehired the staff that had been loyal to him for years before being summarily dismissed and replaced by Helene in his absence. Not one of them. He refused to believe it could be one of them. But the alternatives were even more unbelievable.

He'd thought at first—*wanted* to think—that it had been someone close to Lexi, possibly one of the new staff members, someone who had helped her in her misbegotten escape. That possibility looked more improbable each day. Questions. So many questions. And no one had answers—except possibly Dr. Wilford Hampton, and his contacts had told him he wasn't talking, even though the first of what would probably be many court proceedings was rapidly approaching.

"Lexi?"

A pulse beat wildly in her throat, but she sat tensely still, as one of the birds behind the delicate grillwork might, had he trapped it in his hands.

She'd been gently raised, although too often he had let himself forget that, gently raised and never exposed to the harsh realities of life until only hours before he had torn her from her hiding place in the middle of a South American coup and dragged her with him into a nightmare.

A nightmare he'd only thought they'd escaped.

A nightmare that in the best tradition of horror kept recurring, kept dragging them back into its web.

He sat beside her and took her hand in his. He felt her pulse flutter in her wrist, but her fingers interlocked with his, holding on to him. He expelled a tightly held breath on a silent prayer of thanks for that much, at least.

"Eva told me dinner was unpleasant," he said, watching her closely.

"You might say that." Her eyes closed briefly; her

breath came unevenly. "It seems I'm not as clever or as assertive as I had begun to hope I might be."

"Tell me," he urged.

"Didn't Mrs. H.?"

"No. She only knew that you left without finishing your meal, not what was said to make you do so."

Her hand flinched within his grasp. She turned, only her head, and studied him through shadowed eyes.

"Will you tell me something, please?" she asked. "Just for tonight will you forget or ignore Melissa's warnings and answer my questions? It's important, Richard." She caught her lower lip between small white teeth and worried it for a second. "It's important."

Could he?

As recently as yesterday he might not have been able to, but now... Now he was no longer sure that Mel's path was the only, or even the best, to take. But what path was safe?

# Seven

**"I**'ll try."

Even though she'd asked for it, Lexi heard Richard's reluctant agreement with a sense of dread. He still held her hand. She wondered how long he would want to.

"Why does everyone hate me?"

"Lexi, not everyone—"

He stopped in mid-sentence, unable to finish a statement she knew would have been untrue.

"Maybe *hate* is too strong a word," she said. "And I know you don't. No one could have been as—" she started to say *kind* and realized how bland that word was "—as gentle, and as comforting, as you have been and hate me. But I'm not sure you like me very much sometimes.

"And Eva doesn't hate me. But I'm equally sure she doesn't entirely trust me. But the others... What did I do, Richard? Please tell me what I did."

He didn't answer—of course not—but she felt him tense beside her. "Greg called me a liar and a thief. I can't argue with him because I don't—*I don't know!*

"And tonight—tonight he made a point of talking about hospitals—surgery, therapy, rehabilitation. And us. All of us. Including you. He called us the walking wounded."

"Damn!"

His hand clenched on hers. Now she twisted her fingers in his and gave him a gentle squeeze, scant comfort for all he had offered her in the past, but all she was capable of giving at that moment.

"We are, you know. Greg with his horrible injuries. You with your scars. And me with this big void where my past ought to be. What would cause that, Richard? What horrible thing would black out a person's entire past?

"Please. Please tell me. Am I responsible? Did I some-how—" Oh, she didn't want to know this. Yet she had to know. "Are your injuries and Greg's *my* fault? Did I—"

He still held her hand. She raised her other fist to her mouth to hold back the cry she felt building within her. *Had* she caused the pain that filled this house?

"No!"

Richard grasped her shoulder with his free hand, forcing her to turn toward him. "No," he said again. "Never think that."

A moan broke from her, despite her efforts to stop it. Lexi threw her head back, as she felt the relief wash through her. Far overhead the girders of the glass ceiling met in convoluted patterns, so like her life. So like the emotions that tumbled and rioted within her. But this, at least had been lifted from her. This guilt at least she no longer had to bear. She didn't think she could have continued—what? living?—if she had been the one to cause Richard's pain. Or Greg's.

"Then what?" she whispered. "What?"

"Did someone say that?" she heard Richard ask tightly. "Did someone dare accuse you of causing Greg's injuries?"

"Not exactly." Greg's words had wounded her at dinner. They still had the power to cut deeply. "He said he would have been better off, and that none of the rest of this—whatever *this* is—would have happened, if everyone had done what I wanted and just let him die." She turned to look at him, needing to see the truth in what he answered. "Did I want him to die? Could I have been so unfeeling?"

Richard released her hand and captured her face, studying it with an intensity she had seldom seen in his eyes. "No," he said. "No."

"Then what, Richard?" she heard herself asking again, unable not to, unable to hide the plea in her voice.

He closed his eyes briefly, then hauled her close, hiding her face against his throat. So he wouldn't have to look at her? So she couldn't see him when he spoke? Lexi didn't know, but she knew she wasn't brave enough to fight her way out of his embrace, not when the words she'd asked for had the power to destroy any decent image she had built of herself.

"Greg was at a medical conference in Colombia, South America, at the request of a former colleague, presenting a paper on a new surgical technique. He was kidnapped from the street just outside his hotel by the terrorist wing of a revolutionary group in a neighboring country. As information later revealed, they thought he was—they thought he was someone else. But we didn't know that at first.

"Mel came to me for help in rescuing him. And no, you didn't want me to go."

"Rescuing him? As in going to South America?"

She felt his head nod and a slight tightening of his arms.

"But why would you go? What could you do that—that the authorities couldn't?"

"I had...contacts, Lexi." His words came slowly, painfully. "Contacts from my prior work, when I—spent a lot of time in that country."

Another hidden fact. Why had it been necessary to keep even this from her? But that still didn't explain why he would have gone. "And because you were once a journalist, Melissa expected you to jump into danger?"

Now she did pull away. Slowly she raised her hand to trace the abrasion on his cheek. "And there was danger, wasn't there? You were injured. How badly, Richard? And I didn't go with you. Mrs. H. as much as told me that, and Helene confirmed it tonight. But if I didn't—if I wasn't there, what happened to my memory?"

She shrugged away from him and stood. Pacing to the aviary, she gripped the bars and held on. Even with his admission, nothing fit. Nothing fit.

She whirled to face him. "And how does not wanting you to put yourself in harm's way make me a thief? Make me a liar?"

"Greg had no right to say that."

"Why not? Is it true?"

He rose. He took a step toward her before stopping. But he didn't answer.

"Richard, please tell me. You have no idea what not knowing is doing to me."

"Yes, Alexandra. I'm afraid I do."

He looked away from her, toward the group of furnishings clustered beneath another towering palm. He drew a breath, scrubbed his hand over the back of his neck and threw his head back, looking toward the ceiling as she had only moments ago. There weren't any answers in that ceiling; she could have told him that.

"No. You didn't go with us. Melissa and I flew into Bogota. I left her there, waiting for me to bring her husband back to her. I found him. The small plane in which we were returning to Bogota went down. There was a fire."

His words were terse, economical. She wondered at the horror he tried to leave out of his telling, yet didn't.

"Fortunately, both of us were pulled to safety by a priest from a nearby village. He got us transported to the nearest hospital."

Lexi walked to his side and lifted her hand to his shoulder, sensing that he needed her touch. And even if he didn't, she needed to touch him. He captured her hand and held it against him.

"Helene flew to be with Greg. There was never any doubt of that," he said at Lexi's small murmur of protest. "She told me that, along with other things."

He grimaced. "She also brought me your petition for divorce."

Lexi gasped. He held her hand more tightly, refusing to let her pull it away. "The petition asked for a large settlement, but no larger than I would have given you had you asked me to release you from our vows before I left."

"I divorced you?"

"No." Now he did surrender her hand. He turned to

face her. "You left me. And you took enough of our joint assets to more than meet the settlement demand."

Lexi recoiled from this picture of the heartless creature he had just told her she was. Shaking her head in horror, she tried to back away from him. Again he captured her face in his hands, stilling her. "At least that was what I thought until today."

She thought back on the day, unremarkable, except for the closeness she had felt with him. "What happened today?"

"Today I finally got past the pain, to remember the woman I'd married."

Thank goodness. Today had reminded him of that woman. Did that mean, could that mean, that at last she had a true picture of who she had been?

"But you came for me," she said. "In spite of what you thought I'd done, you came for me."

"Not soon enough." She felt his hands tense on her face before he dropped them. "Not soon enough."

She missed his touch—needed his touch. Not knowing if he would tolerate it, she had to reach out. She lifted her hand to his chest and felt the heavy beat of his heart beneath his sweater. Strength and softness: the contradiction that was Richard. So many questions. So many answers that told her only that there must be more—much more to learn. "Does this mean—"

"Please, Lexi. Don't ask me more. Not tonight."

"Then, when? There's still so much to know. Where was I, Richard? What happened to me? You think I wouldn't have left you, but I did? Why? Where did I go? Why did I try to divorce you? It makes no sense. Why can't I remember? *What* can't I remember?"

"What you can't remember is that you never loved me."

Her hand clenched on his sweater.

"That you married me out of a sense of gratitude and because at that time you had—I gave you—no other options."

"No. I can't believe that. Not now. Not knowing you."

"But you were never cruel," he said. "Never dishonest. And I thought for a while that you were happy, or as happy as we could be in the enforced isolation of this house."

"And you, Richard?" Her breath shuddered from her as she held back a moan, not wanting, not able to believe his words. But why would he lie? "Did you love me, or were you, too, out of options? And were you happy?"

"That's all I can tell you now, Lexi. More than I should have."

"Richard—"

"It's late, Lexi. It's been a long day, and tomorrow promises to be longer. Let's go to...to our rooms."

To bed he'd almost said. She saw it in the clenching of his jaw and the tension in his arms and felt it in the heat radiating from his body. Once he would have said it, she knew that now with a certainty she hadn't felt before. Yes. She had lain with him, and in spite of his words she had loved him. She knew that, too. But why didn't he? Had she never told him? So many questions. Too many. And each answer only brought the need for more.

She didn't want to go back upstairs but now not even the conservatory provided her a haven. There was no haven for her. Yes. Yes, there was one. But Richard seemed determined to deny her that, except as some helpless needy invalid. But she wasn't an invalid. Not anymore. Only her memory was faulty, not the part of her that thought and felt and loved. And somehow she would have to convince Richard of the words he had spoken only that morning—convince him that even without her memory, even without the knowledge that he withheld from her, she was his wife.

She released her grip on his sweater and stepped back. "Yes," she said. "Let's go upstairs."

Lexi had the dream again. Not the one about stairs and disabled telephones that left her heart racing and her body drenched in a clammy sweat, but the other—the one that only recently made itself known to her. Richard. Her dark angel. Bearded. Tougher. Standing shirtless in front of a window in a stark bedroom. She woke up just when Lexi in the dream wrapped her arms around him and rested her cheek against his back.

Never loved him? She had loved him. Lexi knew that. And she had made love with him. In her dream. And here, in the bed they had shared.

*If I told you that you loved me beyond reason, and the two of us were happier here than any two people had a right to be, you'd believe me?* Lexi remembered the words he had spoken the night he returned her to this house. She had wanted to believe him then. *Or if I told you that you feared me, that you hated this place, that you only waited for a chance to escape, would you believe that?* Was that what he wanted to believe? Or had she given him reason to do so?

The wind whipped up outside her windows readying itself, she was afraid, for another bitter storm. This house was so cold, so cold, in spite of the wealth that built it, in spite of the massive boiler in the basement, in spite of the multitude of fireplaces that kept the staff running to fuel and clean and tend them.

And Richard had grown up here. Grown up in a house that had no nursery, no playroom, no space for a child to be a child. How cold had it been for him with a mother who had loved only the house, not those it should have sheltered. Could it be that Richard was the one who wanted to escape? Or that the escape he thought she wanted had been for both of them?

Richard, standing before a window. Lexi's thoughts returned to her dream. Dark. Dangerous. Alone.

Alone as he was now. As he always was, even when he brought her comfort in the night.

Had anyone ever comforted him? Besides the dream Lexi, had anyone ever gone to him, held him, loved him?

And how could she be so certain that no one had, when all of her own life before Boston remained hidden from her?

But she was.

And now he lay alone only a few feet from her, alone because he would not impose himself on her, even though this was his bed, his room, and she was his wife.

She was out of bed and across the room before she realized she had moved. The door between their rooms stood open, as it had each night since he'd returned her to this house—open for her sake, but not for his. In her dream his skin had been supple beneath her touch, supple and heated, and his need had been as great—no, greater than hers.

Lexi stopped in the doorway and looked across the darkened room to the bed illuminated by the amber glow of a shaded lamp.

Richard slept. Even in the nighttime chill of the room he slept shirtless. He had thrown back the blanket and lay on his stomach with his arm stretched up and wrapped around the pillow that cradled his face. For the first time

Lexi saw the extent of the injuries that the abrasion on his face only hinted at.

*There was a fire.*

How dispassionately he had spoken those words.

"Oh, Richard." Her words whispered through the silent room.

She saw him tense and knew she had awakened him.

She could leave. Perhaps he would never know what had disturbed his sleep if she just backed from the room and remained silent. But that was the coward's way, and Lexi feared she had acted in that way much too often.

He sat up, moving his scarred arm and shoulder into the shadows. "Lexi?"

Of course he could see her. The fire still glowed from the hearth in her room. Even so, Richard must have eyes like a cat. Her silhouette could be no more than another shadow in the many already filling this room.

"Yes."

"What's wrong?"

And of course he would think that only her neediness had driven her to his room.

She could lie. He wouldn't find a gentle way to drive her back to her side of the door if she did so. He'd gather her in his arms and console her. But Lexi didn't want consolation. For her or, she realized, for him.

"Nothing is wrong." She stepped farther into the room. "Or maybe everything is."

Richard reached for a sweatshirt draped over the foot of his bed. Lexi remembered the feel of soft cotton beneath her cheek as he held her to him, the feel of soft cotton beneath her hands as she awoke to find herself clutching at the safety that was Richard. She understood that he kept clothing within easy reach not for his sake but for hers.

She reached his bedside just as he had snagged the shirt up and began to blindly search for arms and neck. As he did so, he looked not at the shirt but at her, at her eyes, at her expression now visible in the lamplight.

Or maybe it was for his benefit, Lexi thought. Maybe he wanted no one to witness the travesty of his wounds. He had been beautiful—so beautiful. Now angry reminders of the fire he'd so nonchalantly dismissed marred that beauty. And they were angry, violent, and she wondered if they were still too new not to be painful.

"If you're covering yourself because of me, please don't."

Richard's hands stilled. He dropped the shirt but continued to watch her as she reached the side of the bed, as she hesitated, as she sat beside him, facing him, close enough to touch him. She didn't do that. Not yet. But she did fill her other senses with the nearness of him.

"They don't...offend you?"

Now she did lift her hand and lightly placed her fingers against his shoulder. So different from the sensation of her dreams.

He flinched when first she touched him and then remained still and stoic under her examination, waiting...waiting for what? She traced her hand across to his heart and felt his life beating, thudding beneath her touch.

"I dreamed about you."

She felt him start to reach for her and used her hand against his heart now to hold him away.

For now. Only for now. This wasn't the touch she wanted from him. She wasn't a needy supplicant. He had to see that. He had to.

She glanced again at his wounds and knew his gaze followed hers. "This wasn't a part of you in the dream, but it doesn't change who that person was."

She felt the catch of his breath and heard his hastily muffled moan.

"And who was that person, Alexandra?"

"Someone I loved very much, even though you didn't believe me."

Richard captured her hand and held it pressed to his heart. "It was a dream, Alexandra."

"Was it? Or was it memory?"

Amazing. He wasn't demanding she recount every instance of this dream the way he had of all the others.

"My hair was long," she told him. "Past my waist. Yours was long, too, and you wore a beard."

He tensed beneath her touch.

"Only a dream, Richard? Or is this part of a memory?"

"Go on." No. Not a demand. More like a plea.

"You were my first lover," she said. This was hard. She sensed she had never been comfortable with sharing intimate secrets, but if she couldn't share them with the man she had once sworn to share her life with, what hope could there be for her. And as unlikely as what she was about to admit seemed, she knew it had to be true. "I— I believe I must have seduced you."

He closed his eyes, blocking this avenue to his thoughts, but not the reaction of his heartbeat beneath her palm.

"Only a dream, Richard? Please don't tell me that."

He opened his eyes. They were opaque in the darkness. Stark with longing and denial. "Don't do this, Lexi."

But of course, she must. If there was ever to be any hope for them, or for her.

"This morning at the lake when you kissed me, I knew your touch. I knew your scent. I knew your taste.

"I wanted you," she said. "And you wanted me."

And then, because he made no move toward her, and because the memory of the dream gave her a courage she wasn't sure she would have had without the dream, Alexandra did what she had wanted to do almost since the moment of walking into this house, perhaps even longer if she were truly honest. She bent forward, closing the distance between them, and brushed a light kiss across his abraded cheek before finding his mouth and his warm, shocked and then willing lips with hers.

She heard him moan again, this time not hiding it from her, before his hands came up to clasp her shoulders and he pulled her closer, against him, and took control of the kiss.

Or maybe not.

There didn't seem to be much control in either of them. She felt the tremor in his hands, the desperation in the way his mouth moved over hers, the ragged intake of his breath and the galloping pace of his heart, and knew her own hands, mouth, breath and heart were no more steady, no more calm.

She lifted her hands to his shoulders, knowing she must touch him, must let him know that she *wanted*— no, needed—to touch him. With very little pressure she tumbled over with him until he lay beneath her on the bed, and his hands slid down, holding her to him, molding her to him.

"I want you," he said. "Night after night I've held you and fought wanting you."

And he was fighting it now. Lexi realized the inevitable signs of withdrawal. Why? *Why?* But she wouldn't ask. Not now. Now he might tell her, and this was not a night for secrets she was afraid she couldn't face.

"Don't fight it, Richard," she said, planting tiny,

needy kisses on his lips, his throat, his chest. "Please. Don't fight me."

"I can't," he said, his words strangled and distant. "God forgive me, I can't."

He rolled her beneath him, then fought to free them both from the tangle of covers, the long nightgown she wore and the soft cotton sweatpants he wore. She lifted herself to help him. When he tossed her gown to the floor and pulled her again beneath him she felt the tantalizing pleasure of the weight of his chest against her breasts, the welcome abrasion of his slightly hair-roughened legs against hers, the incredible heat radiating from him, and his undeniable need for her.

He was ready for her. And she—she felt as though she had been ready for him forever. Lifting her hips slightly, she urged deeper contact.

He arched away from her. "Not yet, Lexi. Not...yet. Let me make this good for you."

"It is good, Richard," she managed to say. "And I need you. Now, Richard. Please now."

He shuddered once, and she feared he might pull away, but with a sigh he lowered himself to her, carefully, almost fearfully, joining their bodies.

Lexi let out a long sigh at the welcome and treasured possession. Yes. Oh, yes she knew this touch, hungered for this touch, needed this touch as much as she needed food and air.

*Oh, Richard, Richard, my darling,* she thought again, as she had that morning, but she didn't, couldn't—somehow sensed she shouldn't—say the words *I've missed you.*

And then he did lose control, and so did she, lost in the sensations, familiar and overpowering, that welcomed her back to the haven she knew, but still did not remem-

ber. A haven that Richard had always created for her, a
place and a series of sensations that not even the dream
Lexi had fully experienced. Richard's love, still not spoken, poured from him in every brush, every touch, every
stroke. Lexi felt full to overflowing with it, safe within
it. And she felt able, because of it, to return it silently
with every breath she took, and every response she made
to him. Finally the world faded from around them, leaving them once again secure, sated, and together. Oh, yes.
Finally. Together.

She didn't remember.

Lexi lay in Richard's bed with his unmarked arm
around her and his unmarked shoulder beneath her cheek.
He'd pulled the sheet over them to protect her from the
chill, although how anyone lying next to his incredible
warmth could be chilled, Lexi had no idea.

How anyone could share and remember such soul-
shaking intimacy and not remember the details, only the
emotion, Lexi had no idea.

She didn't remember.

She thought surely something should have come back
to her. A blinding revelation of all that had gone before.
A slow easy awakening to her past as slowly she awoke
to the sensations around her following the cataclysm of
emotions she and Richard had just shared. A glimmer.
An idea. A flash. Something. Anything.

Nothing.

She felt Richard's fingers brushing across her cheek
and the moisture there.

"I'm sorry, Lexi."

"Don't say that." She caught her rising voice and her
rising hysteria. "Don't *ever* say that, Richard. Don't take
this from me, too."

His arm tightened around her.

"We're married," she said. "You told me that. And we were lovers. In the room next door. In the bed next door. I *know* that."

"You remember." Later she would give herself time to wonder about the flatness in his voice. Later. Not now.

"No! I should. I know I should. But I don't. All I know is that I need you Richard. Not just as a comforter in the night. Not just as someone in the next room. Not just as a sometimes answerer to my too-many questions."

She felt the tears on her cheeks now, wet and cold and unstoppable. "I need you, Richard. The way we were tonight. The way we were in our dream. And I don't know what I've done to drive you away."

"Oh, Lexi." He turned, enfolding her in an embrace that was comfort and love and desperation all entangled. "We can't do this again. Not until I— Not yet. Not yet. But, God help me, I need you, too. Let me hold you. Let me…let me love you. Just tonight."

# Eight

Lexi awoke alone.

Richard had tucked the covers around her and had brought her robe from the room next door and draped it over the foot of the bed, but he'd left her.

Feeling vulnerable, Lexi shrugged into her robe and sat up on the edge of this strange bed, trying but failing to hold on to the magic of the night.

This room was starkly elegant, with the unmistakable touch of the redecorating that had been started, but without the finishing touches that would have made it truly Richard's room.

But it wasn't his room, was it? At least, it hadn't been until something had ripped apart the fabric of their marriage. Would she have run from him? *Could* she have run from him? And why? *Why?*

Across the room, a black multiline telephone sat on a table that also held a lamp, a calendar, a pen set and a large, desk-top blotter. One light on the telephone blinked red, drawing her attention, holding it, mesmerizing her until she saw not just the one telephone, but a row of them, dozens, all blinking, all with their cords severed and dangling.

Lexi shook her head, clearing that vision, but she was unable to clear the tightness that had suddenly wrapped itself around her heart. Too late she remembered to try to grab the vision, to try to call forth a memory. Too late she acknowledged that here, in all its bizarre symbolism, must be a clue to what had happened, and she had once again failed to hold on to it.

Shivering from the physical chill in the room as well as from the menace from the unknown, Lexi glanced away from the desk. On the table beside the bed, a small travel clock sat facing away from her. She reached for it and turned it toward her.

No wonder she was alone. For a moment she looked at the clock, appalled at how late she had slept. Then, because that memory brought back the magic of the night, she sat there a little longer, wishing but not sure for what she wished and, startling her, mourning, but not sure, either, for what she mourned.

She was still sitting there when she heard the hallway door open. She looked up in alarm, not sure who would dare enter this room, or why, or even how she should act on being caught in her husband's bed.

Richard stood in the doorway, dressed again all in black, with the worst of his scars hidden by the long sleeves and high neck of his sweater.

He watched her silently for a moment, this man who had pleaded to hold her but who now seemed not to know what to say to the woman who had come to him in the middle of the night. The woman who had—Lexi choked back a moan—who had pleaded with him to hold her, to take her, to love her. Maybe he had nothing to say to her. Maybe all he felt for her now was revulsion. He'd answered none of her questions last night. Not a one of them.

She released her breath and nodded toward the telephone, suddenly, in spite of its menace, the safest topic she could find. "It's blinking," she said. "Does that mean someone should tend to it?"

He stepped into the room and closed the door, leaning back against it. "Yes."

He didn't move toward her, didn't offer her any welcome or censure, any clue to what he felt. "Why don't you get dressed while I do so," he said finally. "Then we can go down to breakfast together."

Her robe was heavy and warm and covered her from throat to toe, but Lexi felt totally exposed as she rose from his bed and crossed his room. For whatever reason, he wanted to deny what they had shared, and she knew she must let him. She paused at the door to her room, giving him this much. "You don't have to do this," she said. For a moment she saw the needy, loving man who had held her in the night, but only for a moment.

"Yes," he said. "I believe I do."

There was no time to savor the changes she felt in her body, no time to remember the delight that had caused them, no hope of retaining the closeness she had felt to Richard. Lexi hurried through her shower and dressed quickly. When she returned to Richard's room, she found him seated at the desk. The light on the telephone no longer blinked, but he held his hand on the receiver as though he had just replaced it. He sat with his head thrown back, as she remembered seeing—when? before.

Sometime before. His eyes were closed. His brow was furrowed as though he were in pain.

"Richard?"

His eyes opened, and he met her troubled appraisal with one of his own, equally troubled.

"Do you trust me, Lexi?"

"Yes." Her only doubt was in the reason for his question.

"Good. I need you to trust me. I need…"

He stood and crossed the room to stand looking down at her. So many questions, all unspoken. So many doubts. And yes, so much pain. It was all there for her to see in his eyes. All there, until suddenly it wasn't. Until suddenly Richard was once again the caring but self-contained stranger. "Are you all right?"

Lexi felt color staining her face. *Now* he would ask her that? Now when all traces of their former intimacy were gone. No. Not quite. The bed still lay in tangled disarray. Perhaps she should tend to it before they went downstairs so that he wouldn't be embarrassed that the housemaid might know what they had done.

*Stop it!*

Lexi screamed at her rioting thoughts. Richard had done nothing to make her feel that he was ashamed of her or what they had shared. *Nothing.* And if he was uneasy with what to say and how to act the morning after, well, she understood that. So was she. She jerked her head in a quick affirmative nod.

He touched her cheek then—just a fleeting, tentative caress. "I hope I never give you reason to hate me, Alexandra, but there are things I can't explain. Not yet."

"Richard—"

He took her arm. "Let's go," he said. "We're entitled to a few minutes before the rest of the family arrives."

\* \* \*

The table had been set for all of them. The sideboard held steaming chafing dishes as well as baskets of bread and trays of fruit, but only Mrs. H. waited in the room. Richard seated Lexi at the chair to his right, and himself at the head of the table. Lexi glanced around and was unable to suppress a shudder. A family meal in all its glory was not the way she wanted to start, or end, any day in this house. But it seemed inevitable.

Mrs. H. poured coffee for them, and then, at a nod from Richard placed a small portfolio on the table beside his service plate and left the room.

"If I could grant one wish for you—short of restoring your memory, which isn't in my power—what would it be?"

Lexi met his serious gaze. This wasn't an idle question but one steeped in a history she might never know. A wish. One wish? That he love her? No. No, that must come from him, not from only her wish. She felt the emptiness of the table to her right and knew that soon it would be filled with people who felt only animosity for her. Get rid of his family? No. That would only hurt him. A wish. One wish. And the words came from a well within her, without her conscious thought.

"Something to do, Richard. Something to fill my days so that I don't constantly—" She broke off. There was no point in traveling that road now. "Something meaningful to do."

He nodded. She saw his strong throat convulse and knew she must have answered as the wife he remembered would have. For a moment she felt a prickle of anger but pushed that away, too. Was he testing her? Or had she somehow already passed a test and this question simply confirmed it? She might never know. Asking him would do no good. Or would it?

"You don't seem surprised."

He smiled then, reluctantly, briefly. He closed his hand over hers where it rested on the table beside her cup and then released her. "No. I'm not. We've had this conversation before. You answered the same way at that time, too. But then, I believe you already suspected that, didn't you?"

Oh, my. An answer.

"And what did you say to me then?"

He moved his hand to the portfolio beside him. "I said, I'm not sure how meaningful this work would be, but if you wanted to make an effort to turn this pile of rock and stone and haunted ego into something resembling a home, I'd be forever grateful."

Lexi sank back in her chair and brought her hands over her mouth, holding them there until she realized that she held them in prayer, in supplication. She looked at the portfolio and then met the questioning regard in Richard's eyes.

He nodded, answering her unspoken question, and handed the portfolio to her. "The dining room was next."

She touched her hand to the portfolio, strangely reluctant to open it. Mrs. H. reentered the breakfast room. "They're on their way."

Richard nodded at the housekeeper and caught Lexi's hand in his once again.

"It may seem—" His voice caught. "It may seem in the next few days that I am using you," he said. "I can't tell you that I'm not, only that if I knew of any other way—"

Voices carried clearly from the adjoining hallway.

"Hell!" Richard shook his head. "I need more time."

But that wasn't to be. Nor was their interruption to be peaceful. Helene's autocratic voice could be heard giving a droll and sarcastic response to something said earlier.

"Trust me," Richard said quickly, softly. "Trust that I will never willingly hurt you. That I will let no one hurt you. Not ever again."

Oh, this was too much, too soon, and all too quickly happening. Trust him? With her life. Yes. Lexi knew she could do that. But what could he mean? How on earth could he use her? And why?

"Lexi?"

She heard the thud of Greg's crutches on the hardwood floor of the next room.

She'd already given him her heart. How much more could her unconditional trust cost her? "Yes," she said. "Yes."

He let out an audible breath, and once again he clasped her hand, but this time she wasn't sure it was for her benefit or assurance so much as for his. She turned her hand beneath his and laced her fingers with his, and that was how his mother, his brother and Mel found them when they entered the breakfast room—sitting side by side, holding hands. Lexi tried to break away, but Richard tightened his grip.

Mrs. Handly busied herself at the sideboard and eventually served Lexi a plate containing a roll and an assortment of fruit.

Helene raised an elegant eyebrow. "Well, I see that your staff can be forced to work when the master is in residence."

Richard looked up at Mrs. H. as she straightened from serving Lexi, and some unspoken message passed between them. "Thank you, Eva," he said. Was Lexi the only one who heard strain in his voice? Mrs. H. nodded and efficiently went about the business of serving the others. When finished she stood back from the table. Richard again looked at her. "That will be all for now."

Mrs. H. set a silver coffeepot on the table in front of Lexi and left the room.

"Really, Richard, you're much too lenient with your domestic staff," Helene said. "I hope this attitude of yours hasn't bled over into your business practices. You have no idea what liberties they take when you're not here."

"Oh, I think I have a pretty good idea of what happens when I'm away."

Helene shot a sharp glance at Lexi.

Then and only then did he release her hand.

"We'll be having guests for dinner this evening."

Now Mel spoke; too sharply, too quickly. "Who?"

"Business associates, Melissa. Two men with whom I've been exploring a number of possibilities."

She raised her eyebrows and glanced warily at Lexi, but said nothing further. She didn't have to. Greg spoke then.

"Damn it! Richard. You know I don't want to meet anyone. That's why I'm stuck here in this mausoleum."

"You don't have to see anyone you don't want to, darling," Helene said. "Surely it won't tax anyone too much to bring you a tray.

"Two you say?" she asked. "Will they be bringing their wives? No. Of course not or you would have said so. Really, Richard, you could have given me more time. I'll have to see to the dining room; it's been neglected horribly. And I'll have to see if your Mrs. Handly has any idea how to entertain in any appropriate manner. Not to mention question her menus and—oh, dear. She does so love to serve early so that she can escape to her quarters."

"Helene. Leave my staff alone."

She stopped in mid-sentence and now the glance she shot Lexi was full of venom. "I suppose you've heard—"

"Enough," Richard told her. "I've heard enough, and I've seen enough."

"But, Richard, someone has to take charge."

Now he did release Lexi's hand. "And someone will. But not you. You are a guest in my house. You are not my hostess. My wife is. And she will determine when we dine and what is served. Is that clear?"

"And where? Richard. If you leave it up to her, she'd have every meal served here, in the breakfast room."

"While you would have every meal served in that graveyard of bad taste down the hall. Well, that won't be an option. Not tonight, and not for some time to come."

He opened the portfolio and took out the top sheet of paper, handing it to Lexi.

"We'd planned to do this months ago. Workmen will be arriving this morning to begin the first phases of the remodeling in there."

"Richard, you can't let her do this!" Helene leaned forward, one hand outstretched toward him. "She's destroying the heart of this house."

Lexi looked down at the plan sheet in her hand, at the simple beauty of the room it revealed. Destroying? Or freeing?

"The heart of this house is filled with cancer," Richard said, and Lexi heard the undisguised bitterness in his voice. "It's long past time for surgery."

"But—"

Richard turned from her to his brother. "And you will

be at the table tonight. I've forgiven you much the last few days because of all you've been through, but I think it's time for you, too, to remember that you're a guest here, and to remember that someone other than you is also in pain.''

Richard sat alone in his office. Alone. With demons he thought he'd faced a long time ago. Now he realized he hadn't faced them; he'd hidden from them. He'd never thought of himself as a coward before. Now he realized that all he'd ever risked was his life, and as everyone knew, that wasn't worth much to anyone, not even himself.

He glanced around his office. Stark. White. Bare of all but the most essential of equipment. Few ventured here. Eva. Jack. In the early months of their marriage, Lexi, who'd been as appalled by this room as she had been by the rest of the house, but for different reasons.

Richard slid open his desk drawer and took out the two photos he kept there.

The first one had been taken the day of their wedding. Lexi had looked ridiculously young to be tying herself to the hardened man at her side, even though she had looked at him with those incredibly luminous eyes of hers and promised to love him regardless of what the future brought. Love? Him? When he'd given her no—had never given her any other option but to bind herself to him.

The second was the photograph he had found in her shoe.

And this was what the future had brought her.

He was positive that the reason given for the depression leading to her hospitalization was a blatant lie. If she had been carrying their child, she had lost it. But not at her own hand. No. Never as a result of her own actions.

Richard leaned back in the chair and closed his eyes as waves of pain worked their way through him. A child. Born of the love he felt for Lexi. Someone with her grace and quick wit and gentle charm. Someone for him to share the love he had bottled up inside himself for so long. Someone to, without reservation, love him for who he was.

He snapped himself upright in the chair, unwilling to let himself get mired in the pain of those thoughts.

Not when there was still so much to consider.

He wasn't so sure that Lexi had voluntarily admitted herself to the hospital. He wasn't sure, in fact, that she had admitted herself.

He glanced at the picture that had finally been returned to him by the most diligent lab in the country with no clue having been found as to its origin. He'd hoped it had been taken from outside the conservatory with a high-powered lens shooting through the glass walls, but it appeared from microscopic examination that wasn't the case. Which meant it had to have been taken from inside the room.

He'd hoped his contacts would discover that someone in his past had tracked him down and taken revenge on those he loved. Greg's kidnapping in South America, after all, had been misdirected vengeance against him. But it didn't seem that this was to be proven. It didn't seem as though there were any way to get around the doubt, the suspicion, the fear, that someone in this house, someone he should have been able to trust, had committed acts of unspeakable evil against an innocent. But then, when had he ever been able to trust anyone?

Alexandra's father—Tom Wilbanks. Yes. He had

trusted Tom. With his life. And Tom had trusted him with what he loved most in the world: his innocent daughter.

And Lexi was innocent. He had to believe that. He'd let himself forget, let himself be swayed by his pain, let himself ignore that there were decent, trustworthy, loving people in the world.

He shouldn't have made love to her. Shouldn't have given in to the need that still racked his body. Not yet. Not until he could come to her free from all doubts about her.

Or all guilt.

*Don't let what you want to see blind you,* Melissa had said to him. More than once. But he had. He'd let his pain and sense of betrayal blind him. And now, if he wasn't careful, he'd let his need to believe in the sanctity of his less-than-sanctified family blind him. And he couldn't afford to do that. Not if it meant endangering Lexi even further. Or himself.

Well, the men who were arriving today, ostensibly to work on the remodeling—who should already be here—would help. It wasn't an agency job. But then, the agency wouldn't have worked it the way he needed it worked. And the men who came would have reported to others, not to him. So his volunteer staff of former co-workers was just fine with him.

And the men who would come to dinner tonight—Richard knew that, for himself, he no longer needed their confirmation. But the courts—if matters went that far—would need it. And somehow, in some way, they might have information unknown even to themselves that would help solve this puzzle.

He glanced at his watch. Time to leave. Should he take Lexi with him this day? Would she be safe here without him? He pushed up out of his chair and shrugged off his vague uneasiness. Her safety wasn't the reason he wanted her by his side; his need was. And his need was what had put her in this hell her life had become. She was safe here; he'd seen to that. Much safer than she would be with him.

Lexi shivered in spite of her heavy sweater, wool slacks and bulky socks. Was this house ever warm?

She had retreated to the library, where Jack had taken time to refresh the glowing fire, and Eva had paused long enough to bring her a pot of tea before leaving her with a pile of books to explore and an afghan to wrap around her legs.

And Richard was gone again. If not out of the house yet, at least away from her. And from whatever drove him? She'd hoped... After last night she'd hoped for a greater closeness with him. But that, apparently, was something he wouldn't let happen.

Now she hid in a book. Or tried to. Only none of the books she pulled from the shelves of this room had the power to wrap her in their world and take her out of hers.

She needed something—anything—to do.

Richard had given her a job, of sorts, but one that didn't require any effort from her.

A job that only earned her more of his mother's displeasure.

A job that had Greg smirking in some sort of self-satisfied undisclosed knowledge.

A job for which she was only in the way of the newly arrived hard-edged, hard-eyed workmen who seemed to find their way into all parts of the house.

A job. When what she wanted was...what?

Not to still, after all these weeks, not know who she

was, where she had come from, and why Richard wouldn't believe she loved him.

And why should he?

Why should Richard believe anything this wimp of a person she was told him? The most assertive thing she'd done in the life she remembered was to go to him last night.

She could hide here in the library, whining to herself about having nothing to do, about having no memory, about needing something to happen to restore...what?

The truth was, something had already happened—obviously something terrible—to bring all of them to this sad, dreary state. Why on earth would she sit around, moaning for something else to strike.

She dropped her feet to the floor and tossed back the afghan.

Could she? Should she?

How could she not?

Lexi found Eva Handly seated at the long pine table in the kitchen, once again sorting through recipe cards. With a quick shake of her head, Lexi stalled the woman's attempt to rise and sat across from her at the table.

Eva handed her a sheet of paper on which she had penciled a tentative menu. "I thought this might work for the meal tonight."

Lexi glanced at the list of tempting and tantalizing foods and knew she should take a greater interest in this woman's loving plans. "It looks fine," she said. "Mrs. H.?"

Eva sank back against her chair. "You're going to ask me, aren't you? You've got that set to your chin. And you know good and well young Mrs. Knapp has told all of us not to say anything to you."

"I think I have to."

Eva sighed.

"There's no one else. Melissa has convinced Richard that silence is to my benefit. I asked her for hypnosis. She refused. Mrs. H., I have to know. Richard says that I'm not responsible for what happened to him and Greg, but I know there has to be some connection between their injuries and my lack of memory."

Eva slid the recipe cards into one neat stack and looked at them, not at Lexi, for several seconds. She bit at her lower lip, sighed and raised her eyes. Lexi saw in them the same confusion she so often felt. "I can't tell you," Eva said.

Lexi slumped in her chair.

"Except—except to believe what Richard says. He'd never do anything to harm you. If he thinks this is what must be done...well then, I have to accept that."

Loyalty. If Lexi had ever had this woman's loyalty, she had lost it by her own actions. She fought back the pain that that thought caused her and eased from her chair. "Thank you, Mrs. Handly," she said in the strongest voice she could muster. "I'm sorry I put you in the position of having to defend yourself or your actions."

# Nine

Lexi dressed that evening in a simple long-sleeved dress of luxuriously soft blue wool she found in her closet. For meeting Richard's business associates, she had experimented with the makeup she found on the dressing table. Amazed and a little frightened by the sophisticated woman who had stared so briefly at her from the mirror, Lexi had removed that makeup in favor of the light touch she preferred.

Now she sat near the fireplace in her room, fervently hoping someone had remembered to crank up the boiler in the basement to make sure the rooms downstairs were warm enough for the guests' comfort. As she rubbed idly at the rings on her finger, she caught a tiny laugh. As mistress of the house, that was probably her job. What a poor chatelaine she made; she'd much rather hide here in this pleasant room than face Richard's family and the unknown men she must now welcome.

"Lexi?"

*Oh, Lord.*

Richard hesitated in the doorway between their rooms. Richard? Hesitant? But he was, and obviously so. Why?

She stood and felt the wool of her dress shift and drape itself around her.

"You look lovely," he told her.

So did he. Oh, so did he. Her dark angel.

Wait. That was—that was the dream Lexi's term, not hers. The dream Richard's description, not...not *what?* And wasn't this Richard her angel? Hadn't he held and protected her? Hadn't he rescued her from whatever had taken her memory? Yes. Yes of course he had. Something had harmed both him and her. Something that was neither her fault nor in her control. She had to believe that. Had to.

"Thank you. Is it time to go downstairs?"

He crossed the room and took her hands in his, holding them lightly as he looked into her eyes. "I'm with you tonight," he said.

*You won't face them alone* remained unspoken, but almost audibly followed his words.

Lexi smiled at him, knowing he needed her courage as much as she did. "Then let's go greet your—our guests."

Downstairs, with Richard beside her, Lexi greeted the three men who had arrived instead of the two she expected. Jack Handly had donned a dark suit and served cocktails and canapés in the reception hall, where the conversation was a little stiff as strangers attempted to find general topics of conversation.

Lexi wondered about the business these men had with Richard, because none of them mentioned it, but she wouldn't let herself wonder why each of them seemed so interested in her. They were discrete in their examination, but she felt it just the same. Or had she just become paranoid, living in the almost constant hostility she felt in this house?

Paranoid. But safe tonight. Because during the predinner drinks Richard did not leave her side, and in the relaxed formality of the smaller room for dinner, sitting next to him rather than at the opposite end of the table seemed natural.

Relaxed formality. Not casual. No. Far from casual.

Dinner was served by two uniformed and competent young women as unfamiliar to Lexi as the men who had invaded the house that morning for the renovations. And she found she was not the only one who had dressed for dinner. Regally beautiful and icily aloof after one pointed stare at Lexi to express her continuing displeasure over the choice of the room, Helene sat in the chair at the end of the table. Mel, equally beautiful, seemed distracted rather than aloof, and between them, Greg with his ravaged hands and pain-stressed face seemed oddly quiet and introspective.

Even Richard seemed strangely tense and waiting. Whatever business he had with these men remained as much a mystery to Lexi at the end of the meal as it had at the beginning, but perhaps that was his plan, because at the end of the meal he glanced at his guests, who each met that glance with either a slight nod or a tiny, negative gesture. "I believe we have coffee waiting for us in the library."

"Business, Richard?" Helene asked. "You don't mean to drag these men from their meal into a stuffy conference, do you?"

Richard looked down the length of the table at his mother. "Yes. Unfortunately I do," he said evenly. "I hope you will excuse us."

"Well, thank God." Greg threw his napkin onto the table and pushed up from his chair. Without another word, he struggled into his crutches and made his painful, noisy way from the room. Mel stood, watching his progress. Helene, not hesitant at all, also rose and after a negligible attempt at protocol followed her son. Mel turned to Richard. "Do you need me for anything else?"

Richard closed his eyes briefly. "No. Go to him, Mel."

She did. But she stopped by Richard's chair and put her hand briefly on his shoulder. "I hope you realize what you may unearth," she said.

Lexi sat trapped, caught in the vision of their two heads so close together. Richard's, dark; Mel's, fair. Familiar. So familiar. But from when? Or where?

But the image was gone in an instant. Mel straightened and nodded toward the men. "Please excuse me," she said. She seemed to address the tallest of the strangers, a quiet man who had spoken very little but had been intense in his examination of Lexi. "I'll be available if you need me later."

"Shall I leave you, too?" Lexi asked.

Richard captured her hand when she would have risen. "No. No, stay with us, please."

The library seemed warm and inviting, with a fire gracing the fireplace and soft lamps lit. Jack Handly waited there, with coffee and brandy, and Eva, absent during the meal, waited with him. With his hand at the small of her back, Richard guided Lexi across the room to the deep leather chair she so often chose and stood beside her after she was seated, resting his hand on her shoulder. At a nod from Richard, Jack shut the hall door.

Eva stepped forward and began passing cups of fragrant coffee to the guests. When she reached the youngest of the three, he took his cup and smiled at her. "Eva. It's good to see you again."

Eva glanced sharply at Richard, who nodded.

"It's good to see you again, too, Dr. Wilson," she said.

*Doctor?* The man had been here for hours. Why only now was his profession being made known? And the others? Lexi felt herself tense, felt Richard's hand tighten on her shoulder, and then forced herself to relax. Richard had asked her to trust him, and trust him, she would.

With a glance at her and what she could only interpret as an apology in his eyes, Richard relaxed his fingers on her shoulder. "Alexandra, I know you have questions about the past. I know you've been frustrated at my lack of answers. Some of them, I just didn't have. I hoped these men could help us find those answers, together."

Lexi glanced at the three men seated nearby. "You're not business associates, then?"

Richard shook his head. "No. And I'm sorry for the charade."

The third guest, a round, elflike man, wearing a suit that must have cost the earth, grimaced. "Well, Jordan, under the circumstances, I can see why you thought it necessary."

Trust was one thing; remaining in ignorance, another. Lexi studied each of the men as carefully as they had once studied her. "Do I know you then? Have you been a part of my life?"

The one identified as Dr. Wilson smiled at her. "Only briefly, Mrs. Jordan. I treated you last spring for a bad case of bronchitis and…and a minor gastric infection."

She looked at the tall one, the one Mel had seemed to speak to, the one identified earlier as Everett Jones. "And you? Do I know you?"

He shook his head but didn't smile. "I'm a psychiatrist. Occasionally I confer with Dr. Knapp—Melissa. You and I have never met."

So what was he doing here? Examining her as a patient? Lexi wasn't sure she wanted to know. "And you?" she asked the one she thought of as an elf. "Are you a doctor, too?"

"No, dear." All traces of humor fled from his expression as he answered her. "My name is James Harrison. I too am sorry for the charade, but we felt it circumspect not to announce my true identity earlier. I'm an attorney. I specialize in divorces, usually high profile and always high dollar. Some months ago I filed a divorce action for an Alexandra Jordan against Richard Jordan."

Lexi drew back against the chair as his words hammered at her. So she had done it then? Betrayed Richard as everyone seemed to think.

*"No,"* she whispered. "I didn't. I couldn't have."

"No, my dear, you didn't. I don't know who the woman was. She bore a strong resemblance to you, but I can honestly say I've never seen you before in my life. And I've got to figure out what I can do to rectify this situation."

She felt the tension return to Richard's hand as he gripped her shoulder and raised her hand to cover his.

Lexi didn't know what answer she had hoped for with her murmured protest; this certainly wasn't it. "Someone else?" she asked. "Someone lied about being me? Who? Who would do such a thing? Richard? And why?"

"I don't know."

Richard didn't know. Well, if he didn't, who did? And why on earth had it been necessary to keep her in the dark about the purpose of this visit? Unless—unless Richard had believed that she might be a woman who could have treated him with such contempt. But of course. He had.

"And you?" she turned her head toward the psychiatrist, Dr. Jones. "Are you here to examine me? Or identify me?"

Everett Jones lifted his left eyebrow and studied her openly now. "A little of both, Mrs. Jordan."

Anger. After weeks of fear and confusion, anger felt healthy and a little heady. Yes. Anger. Lexi felt it growing, but she wouldn't give it free rein. Not yet. "And did I pass inspection?"

He gave her a brief, wry smile. "More so each minute."

Lexi paced the floor in front of the fireplace in her bedroom—back and forth, back and forth—feeling the room close in on her. A prisoner? No. She refused to believe that. But the thought kept returning. She glanced at the low table in front of the sofa where a still-full teapot and delicate cup waited. Eva had summoned them as she waited with Lexi, hovering, unsure of herself in the face of Lexi's agitation, until Lexi had all but pleaded with her to leave her alone. Lexi wasn't sure what Eva's purpose had been in waiting, except it had seemed so definite she wondered if Richard hadn't insisted.

Why?

Did he think she would run away again? And what had this entire charade of an evening proved? Anything?

The wool of her dress, fine as it was, chafed at her. Lexi began stripping it off as she made her way toward her dressing room, shivering in the draft from the closed-off sunporch that whistled through the marble bath. In her dressing room, she changed into comfortable jeans and a sweater. If she was going to have this out with Richard, she would be dressed, and have it out she would.

There had been no more answers that evening, and no more time for questions, at least from her. With only a few terse words to Jack and Eva, and an enigmatic glance at her, Richard had left almost immediately with their guests—guests!—to drive them to the airstrip for their brief return flight to Tulsa.

The books were on her dressing table. She found them when she turned to run a brush through her hair. Six of them, big fat hardbacks with glossy covers, had been plopped onto the delicate table in the middle of jars and vials and brushes. Lexi sank onto the gilded stool in front of the table and looked at them warily.

And now the emotion that raced to her heart chilled her neck. Who had been in this room, and—Lexi curbed a bitter laugh—even for her, the question *why?* was becoming monotonous. She touched the top book cautiously. Maybe she shouldn't. Maybe there would be fingerprints or something—

Sure. She would go to her husband, the stranger who had brought other strangers into his house to examine her and hadn't bothered to explain, to ask, to—

The stranger who had loved her with such gentle desperation in the dark of the night.

Lexi closed her eyes and gave in to a moment of defeat. Who was Richard Jordan? Right now the answer to that question seemed as important as knowing who she was.

Sighing, she returned her attention to the books. As everything else in her brief memory, this held another puzzle. She might as well see if this one made any more sense than the others.

They were all by the same author—a name she didn't

recognize any more than she had recognized her own. All were apparently new copies, although the copyright dates were spaced a year apart. All were the type of book she'd term thriller or political espionage, a book she knew instinctively would chill her, and none seemed the slightest familiar. Until she reached the last one, also the latest. The jacket blurb said little, but what it did say stilled her hand and her breath, until she forced herself to continue reading, to turn to the back cover, to see…

None of the others had included an author's picture. This one did: a grainy black-and-white candid shot, taken from a distance. The man in the photo was barely identifiable, dressed in jeans and khaki, wearing several days' growth of beard and with his eyes shaded by dark glasses. He was leaning against a battered, jungle-colored, military truck of some sort.

Barely identifiable. Unless someone had seen him in her dreams. At a window. At night. In a small, spare room. Unless someone had seen beneath the beard and the rough exterior to find the elegant man who had comforted her and finally loved her in the dark of the night, and then betrayed her only hours ago. The man who kept secrets, even about herself, from her. Lexi whimpered. Then she opened the first book and read the jacket notes.

Each was another adventure of a continuing character, a foreign correspondent who made his way through the underbelly of the world hiding his true mission, that of a covert operative of a fictionally named government organization, fighting evil and getting tarred by it as he went, wanting out, not knowing how, long since convinced his work did no real good. Until the last episode, the book that contained the picture she recognized.

And that wasn't all she recognized. No, nothing so specific as memory teased at her, but something called to her. Something tightened a fist around her heart and had her tensing her shoulders, waiting for—waiting for *what?* He—the character, identified only as Dawson—was quitting. Had quit. And then he received word that his former partner's identity and safety had been jeopardized. He found himself thrust back into the danger and intrigue of the world he wanted to escape, this version filled with a South American terrorist organization, a steaming, insect-infested jungle, a partner he reached too late to save and the partner's daughter, an innocent he had to guide back through that jungle to safety.

The house was never completely dark. Discreetly placed wall sconces shed soft light in amber pools throughout all the long hallways, revealing the ornate treasures of a past Richard had long tried to convince himself had nothing really to do with him.

But it was quiet. Quiet as the tomb of all his dreams. Dreams he had for a few brief months begun to think he might be allowed to have.

He had returned from driving his dinner guests to the airport to find the house illuminated only by security lights and a few scattered lamps from within. The dogs patrolled the grounds but approached him when he emerged from the garage. The younger one, the female, came close for a scratch behind her ear and gave a soft whine. "I know, girl," Richard told her. "I miss her, too."

Inside the house, the downstairs rooms were shrouded in shadow, the daytime staff was gone and most of his men were already settled for the night in the little-used servants' wing. Two men still patrolled the dimly lit hallways, as silent and as invisible as the ghostly shadows they had long-ago been trained to be.

Lexi had hated this house from the moment she first saw it. He had brought her here to keep her safe after their escape from the terrorists who had killed her father. And then, when he had failed to do so—as had been so chillingly proven to him tonight—he had blamed her.

A darker shadow emerged from a Jacobean chair as he neared the door to Lexi's room. Eva.

"Is she asleep?"

"I don't know, Richard. She said she wanted to sleep, but she seemed too tense even to rest. Are you sure—I know what Dr. Knapp says, but is it possible—"

"That I've made still another mistake with my wife's safety?" He heard the edge in his voice, thought about fighting it and realized it felt good to let his bitterness show. "I don't know. But Dr. Jones agrees with Melissa's treatment. And perhaps it's better if she doesn't remember anything, at least until the trial is over."

"But that could take months."

Richard shook his head, stopping her protest. "There's a hearing this week. Only the first of many, I'm afraid, but Jones agreed that Alexandra is much too emotionally fragile to testify, even if she had anything to tell. He's going to Boston with us—with Melissa and me. Tomorrow. And Harrison is putting his investigator to work on solving the question of who started the divorce proceedings."

"Was she here, Richard? Was that person in this house? Is it possible that she was the one who fired us and not Lexi? I loved that girl. Shouldn't I have known?"

"Eva."

She visibly controlled herself, pulling her shoulders back and lifting her eyes. "I know. It had to be Lexi. No one else could have come in without *someone* knowing. But I don't want it to have been her."

"I understand," Richard told her. "Believe me. I understand."

When he reached Lexi's room, he found her asleep. Curled in a small huddle on the white sofa in front of a dying fire, even sleeping, Lexi looked far from resting. She had been crying. Drying tears tracked her cheeks and spiked her lashes.

*Good job, Jordan,* he derided himself. He'd really done a fine job of protecting the one person who'd ever come close to convincing him he was loved.

*Was she here? Was that person in this house?*

Eva's suspicions haunted him. They couldn't be valid. The implications if they were, were too horrible to contemplate. But yet—

Quietly he walked through Lexi's bath and checked the door leading from it to the area beyond. Locked. As the one from the hallway leading to that room had been when he'd checked it moments before. As they both had been since he'd telephoned orders from Boston.

He carried the key. For the first time he wanted to open the door, to look from the vantage point of new knowledge at what lay beyond. But he wouldn't. He'd not been into that wing in months, when he'd stormed and cursed and had barely held back a howl of pain at Lexi's betrayal. Why had she begun the renovation in that wing of all places—secretly, not telling even him—and then—

But *Lexi* hadn't divorced him. Had she left willingly? Or had she been taken from him? And if so, by whom? And why? There had been no ransom demand. No gloating by any one of his well-earned enemies. No word of any sort until he'd stumbled across that hidden account with its preauthorized systematic withdrawals.

No. Too many questions remained unanswered for him

to open the door to this particular wing and the potential pain it held.

When he returned to her sitting room, Richard found Lexi still asleep, but now the tears tracking her pale cheeks were fresh. He stood looking down at her, wanting only to gather her in his arms, carry her across the room to the bed they had so briefly—so magically—shared and pretend that most of the past year had never happened.

But it had.

And because it had, he had no right to touch this woman he had taken to be his wife—might never again have that right.

A light wool afghan he'd given her when they first came to this house lay draped across the nearest chair. Lexi had wrapped herself in it every night then, as they'd sat before the fire, chilled, always chilled after the warmth of her tropical home. He lifted the afghan to his face, touching the soft cashmere to the abrasion that marred his cheek. The wool carried the delicate floral scent that would always remind him of Lexi, and its gentle caress was for a moment hers, touching him, healing him, giving him the hope, the prayer, of her loving him.

And he knew that if he lifted her in his arms, she would go with him, would share with him the magic she had given him last night.

And he could not do that to her.

Reluctantly he lowered the afghan from his face and draped it over Lexi's still, sleeping form.

Lexi wasn't sure what woke her, but something did. She lay quietly, watching the fire and listening until she was certain that all she heard was the wind.

Luxurious cashmere wrapped her in its warmth.

Vaguely she remembered thinking she should cover herself with it, but not letting go of her misery long enough to reach for it.

Richard.

Of course.

Caring for her.

Even though his own words had shattered her dream.

Memory?

Maybe.

But of what?

A scene she'd read in a book. Only that.

Lexi scrambled up into the corner of the couch, dragging the afghan with her.

Or was it?

Richard's version had been different—as of course it should have been, told from Dawson's viewpoint. Dawson hadn't believed in her—in the fictional Maria's avowal of love, hadn't believed himself to have any right to love, or any qualities to love.

Lexi had sped through the book appalled and fascinated by the story; drawn to the man, the heat of the jungle, the calls of the birds and pungent aroma of the river; repelled by the portrayal of the violence the two characters endured and escaped. Had she read the book before? Was that what she remembered? But if so, why did only that one scene seem familiar?

This was an answer only Richard could give her.

This was an answer he *would* give her.

As he had the night before, Richard lay on his stomach with his arm stretched up and wrapped around his pillow. She stood beside his bed before he came awake, fully alert and wary.

"Did I ever read your books?"

His eyes clouded in confusion. Well, that answered one

unasked question—*he* hadn't put the books in her dressing room—but that wasn't the answer she needed. Not at this moment.

"I know I'm not supposed to know about them unless I remember," she said softly but with a determination that silenced the question she knew he would ask, "and no, I don't remember. And no, I don't understand why you would hide something as basic as your career from me, but that's not important right now. Answer me, Richard. Have I ever read your books?"

Tense. She saw the muscles in his arm and shoulder bunch and ripple, saw the moment he surrendered to her the right to know.

He released his grip on the pillow and turned on his side, facing her. "No. You hated violence. They were nothing you would ever have wanted to read."

"Even though you wrote them?"

"Especially because of that."

He was wrong, Lexi thought. She would have wanted to read at least that last one.

A memory. A real memory plucked out of the darkness of her past, revealed only in the language of dream. Had the rest of the book basis in her past, also? She might never know. But she did know that somewhere she and Richard had shared the beauty of her dream and that he had chosen to use it as a moment of sanity and a haven in the midst of terror.

It was enough.

For now it was enough.

She reached for the blanket covering him.

"Go away, Lexi."

His voice grated in the shadows of the night.

"Lexi. I'm trying to do the right thing. Please. Let me."

The right thing? Who knew what that was anymore? Had she ever? But at this moment her actions seemed very right to her. She lifted the blanket and slid into bed beside her husband.

"Don't tell me you don't want me here," she said. She placed her hand on his shoulder and felt the tension holding him taut and motionless. "I won't believe you."

He remained coiled and unyielding for a lifetime of seconds before groaning and wrapping her in his arms. "No. I won't tell you that. I never could. Not even when I knew I should."

# Ten

**R**ichard awoke her before dawn by sliding his arm from around her and easing himself out of bed.

Lexi murmured a protest.

"Shh," he told her. "It's all right. Go back to sleep."

Warm and content, sated and wrapped in the love he had shown her but still not spoken, Lexi did. She awakened later to see him dressed in another of his elegant dark suits and leaning over a nearby chair, closing the zipper of a garment bag.

She raised herself on one elbow and tried to make sense of the shadowy scene.

"Richard?"

He stiffened. His hands stilled on the zipper. Slowly he straightened and turned to face her.

"Are you going somewhere?"

She envied him his ability to come completely awake between one beat of his heart and the next; she felt thickheaded and dumb. He hadn't told her he was leaving, had he? Hadn't mentioned a trip, especially not one that would require luggage. Hadn't asked her if she would rather go with him or stay here in this mausoleum surrounded by people who either didn't care about her or actively disliked her. Locked away, like so much—

The warmth that had enveloped her fled, leaving her chilled and suddenly nauseated. *Locked away like so much*—what? Where had that thought come from? The thought, and the awful, mind-numbing fear that accompanied it.

And along with the fear came knowledge so sure she knew it must have been deeply ingrained, that she must not let her fear show.

She sat up. The covers fell away, but the chill of the room was no colder than the chill within her.

"I don't suppose you can tell me where you're going? Or take me with you?"

"Lexi—"

She'd heard his protests and everyone's protests too often—that ignorance was for her benefit—to want to hear any of them again. Especially Richard's, especially after what they had shared the past two nights.

Her robe lay across the foot of the bed. She couldn't hide her quick, jerky motions as she reached for it and shrugged it on.

With a mumbled oath, Richard crossed the room and stood in front of her, trapping her as she tried to rise from the bed. He clamped his hands on her shoulders and held her.

"I *can't* tell you. Believe me, Lexi, this is nothing you want to know. It's nothing *I* want to know. But soon, I promise you, I will tell you what's happening."

"What kind of power does Melissa have over us,

Richard, that she can dictate to you and control almost every facet of my life?''

"You think this is about *Melissa?*''

*Melissa. Perfectly coiffed blond head. Leaning forward. Laughing. And Richard. Laughing, too. "See what he does when you're not around. Do you really think he wants you back? Grow up, little girl. You'll stay here until you rot if you expect him to rescue you."*

Her whimper came from the same dark abyss that had spawned the flash of—of memory? Oh, please, no. She slumped back onto the bed and away from Richard's touch, clasping her arms, holding them against her body. Safe.

"Lexi. What is it?''

She glanced up at him, helpless for now to hide the fear that had ambushed her, and found his frantic, troubled expression, as disturbing as it was, somehow reassuring. But he *had* rescued her, hadn't he? She was here, with him, safe from the indignities of…

Lexi closed her eyes, clamping down on whatever black thing was trying to crawl its way into her consciousness.

"Lexi. Talk to me." Richard grasped her, forcing her to look up at him. "What's wrong?''

He *had* rescued her. He did love her, even if he never spoke the words. And she was safe with him. Lexi had to believe that. Safe. With a small, choked cry she slid her arms around him and held on with all her strength. "Don't leave me here alone, Richard. Please don't leave me here alone.''

His arms tightened and he dragged her up from the bed, against him, so close she felt the racing of his heart against hers. "I have to Lexi.''

"I'll be good. I promise I'll be good.''

Appalled and shocked to silence, Lexi shrugged away from him, noticing only vaguely that he let her go. "I don't know where those words came from, Richard. *Where* did they come from? What kind of person am I that I would beg like that?"

He turned away from her. For a moment, when she saw him throw his shoulders back and his head up, she thought he might answer.

"You'll be safe here, Alexandra." No. He didn't answer her questions. Instead, he answered something she hadn't known to ask, something that only opened to other questions. "I've made this house as much of a fortress as I can. I've taken steps I never thought I'd need, but obviously did need a lot sooner than I realized. I'll return as soon as I can. But I have to go. And I cannot take you with me. Not this time."

In the hours between Richard's leaving and time to dress for breakfast, Lexi subdued her rioting emotions and stuffed back into tidy, well-covered cellars those images that had so disturbed her.

There was a reason she didn't remember her past. After weeks of being told that, she recognized its truth. Whatever had robbed her of her memory was too terrible for her to face.

And did she have to face it? She was free of the terror now. Couldn't she just accept that her life had borne some resemblance to that of the fictional Maria in Richard's last book? Her glimpse of the children, her attraction to the tropical ambience of the conservatory, even her ease and agility in the swimming pool, all seemed to point to at least a life somewhat similar to Maria's. If so, her father, her only family other than Richard, was dead.

Had she grieved for him? Or was that part of what held her memory prisoner?

And what of the telephones and stairs of her nightmares? Couldn't they just be the reaction of moving from a primitive village to this—this crypt of a house?

She finished dressing quickly, in warm, soft wool again, but still the chill penetrated, and a draft teased at her, drawing her through the rooms of her suite until she stood in front of the locked door in her bath.

Locked. Other than the bedrooms when they were occupied, only two doors in this entire house were locked. And they both led to the same wing.

*Dangerous,* Richard had told her. No. What he had said was, *not safe.* Not safe for her to enter. Richard had often *not* told her things, but what he had told her had always been truthful; Lexi had to believe that. She did believe it.

With a shudder she turned from the door. It was time for her once more to run the gauntlet of Richard's family.

Greg and Helene had already seated themselves by the time Lexi arrived in the breakfast room. Helene graced her with a frosty glare but said nothing as she continued with her breakfast.

Greg's face was tight and had that peculiar grayish cast that evidenced the pain that so frequently held him in thrall.

Lexi glanced at the empty seat beside him, and Greg's mouth twisted in a parody of a smile.

"Something else we have in common, Alexandra. I keep telling you, but you won't listen."

Lexi paused with her hand on the back of her chair.

"They're together. My wife. Your husband. Off on another 'necessary' trip."

Her hand tightened on the chair. *Melissa and Richard. Laughing. Intimate.*

"Oh, do sit down and don't be so dramatically tiresome," Helene said as she pushed away from the table. "You can't possibly believe you could hold the attention of a man like Richard. Although I personally don't understand why an educated and intelligent woman like Melissa would prefer him to Greg."

"She prefers him to me because he's a whole man, Mother. Because the bastards who snatched me did this to me instead of him."

"He should have died. He should never have survived that plane crash. You're his brother. We're his only family. Without him—"

"Stop it!"

Lexi's outcry shocked all of them to silence. She clasped her hand over her mouth to hold back words thundering to be said. With a wild glance at two people who should have rejoiced at Richard's recovery, not resented it, she fled the room, to the safety and sanity of Eva Handly's kitchen.

She slammed the door and leaned against it. Eva looked up from pouring coffee for one of the menacing looking men who were there to tear out the old dining room. She exchanged a glance with the man and handed him the cup. With a slight nod in Lexi's direction, he left the kitchen through the service entrance.

"Well, they didn't wait long to start in on you did they?"

Lexi released a quavering breath and straightened away from the door. "Not just me this time," she said shakily. "Richard, too. I thought until now that he was exaggerating, or misunderstanding Helene. But she really doesn't love him, does she?"

Eva shook her head. She reached into the cabinet for another cup, which she filled and set on the table. "Here. Sit down."

Lexi did, and wrapped her hands around the mug, warming them.

"Helene Knapp is incapable of loving anyone."

"Greg?"

"Anyone. As far as I've seen, she has one obsession, and that is this house. Greg is her excuse for being here...she knows Richard won't turn her away from him.

"Just as she knew you wouldn't turn her away months ago when she showed up to wait for news of her sons.

"But none of us knew much about Helene Knapp at that time, other than she was Richard's mother. And like you, I didn't believe she could be so heartless about him. Not then, anyway."

"And Greg?" Lexi asked. "Can he really believe Richard and Melissa are...""

"Greg is in so much pain he doesn't know what to believe. But what about you, Lexi? Don't you know that your husband is, above all things, honorable? He would never betray you, or his brother, by indulging in such an affair."

"Even if they love each other?"

There. The word had escaped and now arrowed and ricocheted across the room, damaging everything in its path.

Eva put her hand on Lexi's shoulder and gave her a gentle caress before turning and walking briskly to the counter, where an array of fruits and breads waited to be served.

"There are many kinds of love," she said as she began assembling an assortment of delicacies. "Many kinds.

Maybe it's time for you to examine just what kind of love you feel for Richard.''

"You do believe that I love him?"

Eva set the plate in front of Lexi. "A blind person could see that you adore him. But do you *love* him? Do you respect him, trust him, admire him, like him, as well as desire him?"

Did she?

But Eva wasn't finished.

"If he were as damaged and hurting as Greg, would you still love him? Or do you only love his strength and the fact that he has rescued you?"

Lexi didn't know. In the two days that followed Eva's disturbing question, Lexi had asked it of herself repeatedly. Solitude gave her a lot of time for questions like that and little opportunity to avoid them.

But she could, and did, avoid Richard's family, even though it meant foregoing the pleasure of the conservatory and pool, and taking her meals in her room.

That morning the weather had cleared, giving her a bright, crisp view of the lake from her room. She'd dressed for extra warmth and made her way to the low balcony which led to the remains of a formal garden, when one of Richard's workmen appeared from, seemingly, no where.

"Ma'am," he'd said, all deference and yet determined to stop her. "If you'd like to walk about the grounds, let me call Mr. Handly to go with you."

She'd seen the dogs then; ears pricked, alert, they'd risen from a sunny spot in the garden and started toward her, and she had hurried back to the dubious safety of the house.

But two days in an elegant suite, no matter how elegant

the suite, was still two days in confinement. Late on the second night since Richard left, Lexi sat on the sofa, wrapped in the cashmere afghan, watching a fire she could not keep blazing high enough to dispel the scrabblings of dark, unsettling and mostly still-hidden images that kept vigil with her.

She had Richard's books with her—all of them—but she hadn't been able to hide in them. Nor could she hide from the fragments of dreams that intruded on her waking hours, of telephones and stairs and now a disembodied voice that accompanied the image of a glass being extended toward her. *Take this. It will calm you. Take this...take this...take this.*

She didn't dare sleep. Because now even *she* haunted her dreams. In a parody of herself, in an older harder version of herself, she preened and examined her reflection in the full length mirror of her dressing room and spoke—to herself—*Do you really think I can't be Richard's wife? Maybe not. But I can be his widow. Never doubt that.* And then she laughed. And Helene laughed, and Lexi moaned.

And the telephone rang—a sharp, persistent, old-fashioned ring—startling Lexi from her unwelcome reveries, but starting her heart racing. It rang. For the first time since Richard had brought her here from Boston. And late—so late at night. *Richard? Had something happened to him?*

She scrambled up from the sofa and across the room to answer it.

"Hello," she said quietly and hesitantly.

"Alexandra." The voice was so similar to Richard's, for a moment she hoped, but so tired, so—defeated.

"Greg?"

He didn't admit or deny his identity, but went on in a

slow monotone, as though he had rehearsed what he must say and didn't dare deviate from his prepared words.

"There's something being rebroadcast on cable news in a few minutes. I've watched it twice already this evening. I know you have absolutely no reason to trust my judgment or my motives, but I think you ought to see this. Will you come down to the game room?"

Greg sat in his motorized wheelchair, a sure indicator that his pain was winning. He lifted a glass in his twisted hand and pointed toward the bar. "Why don't you get yourself a drink, too. I have a feeling you're going to need it."

*Take this. It will calm you....*

Lexi shuddered as the words whispered through her and wrapped her arms around herself. "No. I don't think so. What is it, Greg?"

He nodded. "Probably not such a good idea after all. For either of us." He drank quickly, but clumsily, twisting the glass up to his mouth then holding it close as though reluctant or unable to spend the energy to lower and then again raise it. In his other hand, he held the remote control for the television.

"I hated you, you know. For not wanting Richard to come for me. For being on his mind. I blamed you for distracting him, even for the plane crash—completely illogical, I know.

"I hated him for all the good things about him that I'd once admired—that sense of duty that had sent him after you to start with and had caused the terrorists to come after me, thinking I was him. I hated him for not letting me die in the jungle. And then I hated him for living, more or less whole, while I'll probably never be much better than I am right now.

"And I hated him, and you, for taking my wife with him when he went to fetch you home.

"I did a lot of hating. Hate is an easy emotion. All you have to do is give it its freedom until it destroys you.

"But maybe—just maybe, I have enough humanity left in me to realize when someone else has been as harmed as I have. Maybe even more so.

"I don't know how it happened or why, but my sainted wife's professional opinion be damned. You need to know this."

He fumbled with the remote control, and sound filled the room.

The picture on the large screen television in the far corner of the room focused on an elaborate Georgian mansion set far back from the road, surrounded by an ornate iron fence. As the camera panned the scene, two guard dogs lunged toward the fence, snarling, teeth bared.

Lexi reached for the back of a chair and braced herself against it, behind it. *Dogs. Oh, God. There were dogs.*

The announcer's voice finally resolved into words. "...allegations today that this gracious scene is really a modern-day snake pit, a place for the wealthy to warehouse their unwanted, under the guise of psychiatric care."

The scene cut to a video of Richard and Melissa, both elegant and poised, stepping from a limousine in front of an official looking building.

"...investigation was launched after former international correspondent Richard Jordan reported locating his estranged wife as a patient in this hospital. Dr. Melissa Knapp, Jordan's sister-in-law, who was listed as referring psychiatrist, denies any knowledge of the admission, testifying today that she was out of the country at the time of the admission.

"Jordan's wife is unavailable for comment. Dr. Knapp testified that although now free of addiction, Mrs. Jordan has no memory of her seven-month hospitalization as a result of the drug therapy she received.

"This testimony was corroborated by Dr. Everett Jones, who, acting as friend of the court, recently examined Mrs. Jordan.

"Dr. Wilford Hampton, director of the clinic, claims Mrs. Jordan voluntarily admitted herself. However, reliable information has been received that in at least two other instances, an as-yet-unidentified woman has represented herself as Alexandra Jordan.

"To date, a total of twenty-one patients have been removed to other facilities for evaluation and treatment. Testimony today revealed a decade-long history of forced hospitalization, improper therapy and in many cases erroneous diagnosis...."

Greg again fumbled with the remote, but the following silence in the room was as relentless as the announcer's words had been. He tried to drink, but his hand shook, and a little liquid spilled over, staining his shirt. With a strangled cry, he drew back his arm, sloshing liquid, and hurled the glass toward the stone hearth, where it shattered and the remains of his drink hissed in the coals.

"I'm sorry," he said. "There's not much more I can say. You won't have to hide from me and my acid disposition anymore. Unless, of course, you can't tolerate being around me. I can understand that. I can't tolerate being around me."

The knuckles of Lexi's hand shone white against the chair back as her mind replayed the images. Richard and Melissa. Together. Conferring about something. Laughing. Intimate. *Do you really think he wants you back? Grow up little girl. You'll stay here till you rot....* Her other hand had crept to her mouth and now covered it, holding back her own cry, which she knew if ever she released it would echo Greg's.

She needed to say something, but she didn't know anything at this moment except that she had to escape the pictures and words she had just witnessed.

She forced her fingers to release their grip on the chair and her legs, which seemed as fixed and frozen as her fingers, to move.

"Alexandra," Greg said again. "I'm sorry."

This much she could give him, but no more—she had no more for anyone at the moment, not even herself. "So am I. Oh, so am I."

Lexi had no idea how much time had passed since she fled from Greg and the matter-of-factly reported horror of the television newscast, or how long she had sat on the tile floor of the conservatory, backed against the aviary's metal grate, hidden by the drooping fronds of a low-growing palm.

They would find her; someone always found her.

She'd snatched up a bath sheet on her way through the gymnasium and wrapped it around her. That, along with the heaters hidden throughout the lush foliage and the steam rising from the heated pool should have warmed her, but Lexi didn't think she would ever be warm again.

She hated to grant Melissa anything, but maybe she had been right about not telling Lexi about her past. And Richard? He apparently knew her even better than she had thought. Knowing what had caused her illness brought her no relief, only a sick feeling of disgust.

Lexi scooted back even closer to the metal grate. At least she understood the strange pains and almost unbearable physical demands that had tortured her so, the

intensive medical care she had received, the hazy, helpless quality she had felt those weeks in Boston. Seven
months of addiction to psychotropic drugs would do that
to a person. Yes, they would.

She wouldn't cry. She sensed she had done more than
her share of crying.

She'd begged for knowledge, demanded knowledge,
and now knew she wouldn't explore the knowledge she'd
been given. She didn't want to know, couldn't face
knowing, how she had gotten from this house, with a
sizable amount of Richard's money, if anything was to
be believed, to a psychiatric prison in Boston.

What a coward she was! How could Richard, always
strong, always resourceful, always fearless, stand to look
at her?

She heard footsteps on the tile floor and held herself
very still. The sound of the steps echoed across the room
as they crossed to the grouping of rattan furniture and
stopped. Through the lacy fronds of the palm she saw
Richard's familiar figure, made visible by the watery
lights of the pool. Otherworldly. For a moment, ominous.

So. He had returned.

Richard touched his hand to the back of the chaise,
hesitating for only a moment before he walked to the
concrete bench a few feet from where she huddled—the
same bench they had shared only a few days before.

He stood silently, waiting, before he spoke in a voice
as strained and harsh as…as she had heard before? In a
distant time and place?

"I know you're here."

Yes. He would know. Someone in this house would
have told him.

"I won't hurt you." His voice caught, then continued.
"I promise I won't let anyone else hurt you, either."

She must have made some noise because he stepped around the bench, parted the palm fronds and looked down at her.

"I'm sorry you learned this way."

Of course. He would have talked to Greg.

"You're sorry I learned at all."

"Yes. That, too."

She looked at the hand he stretched toward her—his scarred one, the one he so often tried to hide from her, extended now in still another act of courage on his part. Well, if she couldn't give him courage, she could at least give him honesty.

"I'm sorry I learned it, too."

"I know you have no reason to trust me, Lexi. I promised to take care of you, and I didn't. I have no excuse."

No. Richard wouldn't claim an excuse. Not even dying in the—*almost* dying in the jungle would free him from a promise.

She slipped her hand into his. "Will you tell me why I am such a coward?"

"You're not a coward, Lexi. If you were, both of us would have died with your father. Without your strength and will to survive, we wouldn't be here, now, trying to sort through the fragments of our lives."

His hand clenched on hers, holding her tight, and he drew her to her feet. She thought for a moment he might pull her against him, but instead he took a step away from her, still holding her hand tightly, not letting go.

"Your father never wanted our world to touch you, so he did his best to see that none of the world did. He kept you in convent schools as long as he could. I think he would have been happy if you'd taken vows, preferably with a cloistered order.

"He wasn't happy when you turned instead to secular

teaching in some of the most troubled mission areas of the world. A coward wouldn't have gone where you went to teach.''

"Your book. That much was true, then? He came to be with me.''

"Yes. To protect you. Instead he brought even more danger with him when he was recognized and followed.''

She'd have to grieve for her father sometime; Lexi knew that. But right now the loss was still insulated from her emotions, shaded and softened by the wall her amnesia had built.

"And my mother?''

"I don't know. He never said. Apparently you never knew her.''

Her fingertips rested on his abraded skin. "Then I am truly alone. All I have is…''

He pulled her against him then, folding his arms around her, holding her close against his chest. "Me. All you have is me, Lexi. And all I have is you.''

She wanted to argue with him, to tell him that wasn't true, but she couldn't, not after witnessing how little regard Helene and Greg had for him, not after seeing the bits of his soul he had unknowingly revealed in his books.

"That will have to be enough for us, won't it, Richard?'' she asked. "It is enough, isn't it?'' She hated the quaver she heard in her voice. "Isn't it?''

# Eleven

**R**ichard took Lexi back to his room—not the room they had shared so briefly months ago, but the one where she had come to him, not once, but twice before. He made love with her, to her, with a quiet desperation, knowing he shouldn't, knowing there was no way he could not make love with this fragile, treasured woman who had given him so much but at a cost almost too great to bear.

Later, as she lay sleeping so trustingly beside him, he tried to tell himself that she would have come willingly to him this night. *Now all I have is...you.* Her words haunted him. Would she want him if he told her what the newscast hadn't revealed? The part that he had sworn he would tell her that night? Would she want anything to do with him if she knew that all of the hell she had gone through had been brought about only because she had married him? Or that soon he must decide how to deal with the information James Harrison's investigator had discovered about the woman impersonating Alexandra, or that he would almost prefer to hide that information rather than let Lexi know the truth?

*And all I have is you.* Did Lexi believe him? She hadn't challenged his words. But then, she'd been living for days with the knowledge of how little he meant to the family surrounding them.

*You should have died, Richard. Oh, well. Perhaps you will. Perhaps all is not lost.* God. His own mother had said that to him. When? Before? Or after she had brought that other message, the one that, wrapped in his pain and in the medications he had been taking, he had accepted. Because, in spite of everything he had done to try to convince himself that at last he had found home, haven and love with Alexandra, he had known that the words would come, just hadn't known how or when. *She's left you, Richard. She said, There is no way I can stay with him, now that his body is as scarred as his soul.*

He'd believed her.

He'd accepted her words.

He'd willed himself to die.

But he hadn't.

And if he had died, would Lexi have died soon after? If there'd been no one who knew Alexandra to point out the substitution, would her impostor now be presiding over this fortress of deceit and ego that his grandfather had built?

Or would Helene be? Was she part of the plot that had resurrected an unknown granddaughter of the old man— her niece, to lay claim to the estate. That was the part of the puzzle that they still had to face. Soon.

And who had taken the picture of him and Mel, the one intended to break Lexi's spirit? Helene? Too much pointed to her as the only one who could have done so for him to doubt it any longer, no matter how much he might want to.

Lexi stirred beside him and sighed softly in her sleep.

He'd have to tell Lexi, have to face the revulsion she would try so hard not to let him see when she realized just how much he had failed her, and then he would have to watch her leave.

But not yet. Please. Not yet.

The dim glow of a lamp across the room lit Lexi's face. She was relaxed and at peace as he so seldom saw her. Richard lifted his hand to her cheek and lightly traced the delicate flesh, the determined jaw, the stubborn chin, the lips that had teased and tantalized him and finally brought him almost unbearable pleasure.

She smiled in her sleep and then awoke, slowly, slumberously. "Richard," she whispered, and reached for him.

No. He couldn't tell her. Not yet.

A tapping, persistent and irritating, brought Lexi back from the warm haven of her dream. She felt Richard slide his arm from around her and ease himself from the bed. Early-morning light crept through the windows, which for the moment were blessedly free of the sound of wind, rain or ice hitting against them. Through half-closed eyes she watched Richard shrug into a robe and walk across the room to the hall door.

He slid the lock on the door and opened it slightly, but enough for Lexi to see Mel standing in the hall. The woman started to enter the room, but Richard blocked her way. Mel glanced at the bed, where Lexi lay feigning sleep, and stopped in her efforts to enter.

"How is Greg?" Richard asked.

"Still asleep. I wanted to talk to you before we went any further with this."

Now Richard looked back at her. "Give me a few minutes," he told Mel. "I'll meet you in the breakfast room."

"Richard, in light of what we've learned, I'm not sure that we haven't already waited too long."

"For what, Mel? What's been done is already done. Hurling accusations is not going to change that."

"Nor will waiting," Mel said, "or pretending that there is no longer any danger."

Danger? Lexi tensed at the word. To whom? From whom?

"Fifteen minutes," Richard said in a voice that forbade any argument. "I'll meet you downstairs."

Lexi forced herself to lie still as she listened to the water in Richard's shower, as he emerged from his dressing room, fully dressed in his inevitable black, as he walked to the bed and sat beside her. She called on any acting skills she might have, to pretend that she was just waking. "You're already dressed," she said in a voice that sounded still sleep softened.

"Yes. I thought I'd get a little work done this morning."

A lie. And told with such practiced ease. Had he lied to her before and she just hadn't known?

"It's early," she said.

He touched his hand to her cheek and smoothed a curl away from her face. "I know. And you must be exhausted. Why don't you rest this morning? I'll have Eva bring your breakfast to you."

Lexi watched as Richard left, locking the door as he went, and listened as he tested the lock on the hall door to the blue suite next door.

Was she imprisoned again?

No.

She checked the doors as soon as the sound of his footsteps had faded away. The door to his room opened for her, and so did the one from her suite. She leaned against her door, only then realizing that her heart was beating at a jackhammer rate. Apparently some memories survived, even if not at a conscious level, because she recognized the aftermath of fear in her body's reaction.

And if she wasn't locked in, who, or what, was locked out?

Rest? Lexi didn't think so. Too many questions remained unanswered. And for the first time since waking up in that Boston hotel room, she felt truly awake. Well, maybe only almost awake, because she felt sure there were answers she didn't want to learn and questions she still couldn't face.

*You're not a coward,* Richard had told her, and, oh, how she wanted to believe him. Certainly the woman in his book hadn't been. The fictional Maria had been a fitting mate for Dawson even though he had not always seen it, even though he had felt that his only possible worth to her had been as rescuer.

Lexi felt a moan break from her.

The books were in her dressing room. She gathered them up and carried them to her sofa, where she collapsed among them and hurriedly paged through each book. Dawson's character grew from book to book, revealing himself as increasingly more complex. But each story carried one unmistakable truth, now that she knew to look for it—he thought his only value was that of white knight, no matter how tarnished, as rescuer, protector, defender. And without that role he was, in his eyes, nothing.

"Oh, Richard," she whispered.

True, the books were fiction, but such a theme had to have some basis to recur with such devastating honesty. And Richard himself—he'd gone to rescue her father and saved her. He'd rescued Greg against what had to have been almost insurmountable odds and at great cost. He'd located Eva and Jack and brought them back into the security of his home. He'd come for her even believing she had betrayed him. And now he put up with the painful and irritating presence of his unloving mother so that Greg could heal…and with Lexi's inability to face and get on with her life.

A quick tap on her door was her only warning before the door opened and Mrs. H. entered, carrying a tray. Lexi's first thought was to throw the afghan over the books, hiding them. She stilled her hand. She wouldn't hide again.

Eva set the tray on the table in front of Lexi and knelt to light the fire. She glanced once at the books, and the look on her face told Lexi that hiding the books would have been futile. She was not surprised to see them.

"You brought them to me, didn't you?" Lexi asked.

Eva adjusted the damper on the fireplace and stood, but she didn't respond to the question.

"You couldn't tell me anything—you'd promised not to—but you could and did make sure I'd find answers."

Eva dusted her hands and turned her attention to the breakfast tray. She filled a delicate cup with coffee from the carafe and handed it to Lexi. "How do you feel this morning?"

Lexi sensed more to her question than a simple greeting, and saw in the concern in Mrs. H.'s eyes that there was a lot more that couldn't be hidden from this woman than a half dozen books.

"Does everyone in the house know what happened last night?"

Eva nodded. "Just about. Young Greg finished the job of getting rip-roaring drunk after you left him, and spent a good part of the night tearing up and down the halls in his chair, spewing out some of the anger that's twisted his mind and his heart the past few months."

"And I suppose everyone knows where I was those same months, and why?"

"Alexandra, no one knows *why* you were there, except you and whoever helped put you there."

Lexi dressed quickly after Eva left. Richard had told her she wasn't a coward; it was time for her to start acting as though she believed him.

One of Richard's workmen nodded to her as she reached the main-floor hall. She felt his eyes on her as she made her way toward the breakfast room. Another stepped out of the dining room as she passed, and she felt his scrutiny, too.

Richard wasn't in the breakfast room; neither was Melissa. But Helene sat enthroned at the head of the table, while a harried-looking young woman served her.

She couldn't do it. Lexi knew she'd never have acting skills great enough to pretend that she wasn't afraid of this woman. Helene was—

Helene was what? Vain and selfish, and maybe even evil—how could any mother who wasn't wish her son dead?—but was she truly someone to fear? Yes. Without waiting to examine how she knew that, Lexi went on through the room and into the kitchen. Eva was there, at the stove. But half a dozen members of the household staff were seated at the pine table. All looked up at her in what she could only call alarm. What did they think?

She knew what they thought. That she had spent most of last year in a psychiatric ward. But did they really believe that after the days she had already spent here she would suddenly become violent?

She cast a wary glance at each of them, but although their tension was almost visible, no one seemed anxious to confront her. She shook her head and turned to leave the room, but the door opened, and Richard stood there blocking the doorway. Now what did she do?

"I'm intruding," she said in a steady clear voice. "I'll take my coffee to the library."

There. That sounded reasonable. Richard must have thought so, too. He smiled at her and stepped to one side so she could leave the room. "Eva?" he said.

Lexi didn't wait for the woman's answer. But she did wait for Richard. She had no desire to face Helene again, that morning or any other time, alone. But it seemed that wasn't a problem. Richard's mother had left the breakfast room and her barely touched breakfast. The young woman who had been serving her looked at Richard, nodded, and began clearing the place setting.

"The library isn't a good idea this morning," Richard said as they entered the hall. "I understand you have a fire upstairs. You might be more comfortable there."

"And out of sight," Lexi said, "and away from the speculation of everyone in this house about what your crazy wife is going to do?"

"Lexi—"

Enough. She'd had enough. "Don't lie to me Richard. There are enough blank spots in my life already that you won't tell me about. Don't make me start questioning the little that you do say."

He stopped at the base of the stairway and spun around to face her. "I have never lied to you. Not once."

Lexi sighed and scrubbed her hands across her face, suddenly defeated. "Whatever," she said. "Now, I'll go like a nice little girl up to my room and lock myself in."

He caught her shoulders in his hands. He held her immobile and looked into her eyes, searching as he had so many times before for answers she didn't have.

"Soon, Lexi," he said. "Soon I will have some answers, and then, I promise you, I'll tell you... everything."

She met his regard with one of her own. Did she believe him? She wanted to. Oh, how she wanted to. She nodded once, quickly, and then broke from his touch and fled up the stairs.

The suite didn't feel safe, but neither did it feel like prison. It felt, instead, like a lair for a coward. Answers. She needed answers. Richard had them. And Mel had them.

Mel had them.

Each time Lexi had spoken with her, in her role as doctor, therapist, Mel had taken notes with a fine gold pen on a lined pad. Each time.

And once when Lexi arrived a few minutes early for her session, she had seen a fat file that Mel had almost too casually closed and put away.

Answers. And Mel had gone downstairs, early, with Richard.

Oh, Lord. Should she?

No. The proper question was *Could* she?

The hall was silent and empty when Lexi eased her door open. Would it stay that way?

*You are not a coward.*

Oh, yes, she was. Her heart was beating violently against the wall of her chest.

What if Mel had returned to her room? What if one of the maids was in the room?

All she could do was find out.

Lexi tapped softly on Mel's door and waited impatiently, knowing that at any moment someone could come walking along the hall. When she heard nothing from inside, she tried the knob. It turned in her hand, and the door opened inward. Taking a deep breath, she entered and quietly closed the door behind her.

The housekeeping staff had not yet been upstairs. Melissa's bed remained unmade, though barely disturbed. A quick glance into the bathroom proved it empty, but an unfolded towel was draped over the drying bar, and Melissa's makeup bag sat on the vanity, open but still packed from her trip.

Satisfied that she was alone in the room, Lexi returned to the sitting alcove. Finding the file was almost anticlimactic. Melissa's briefcase sat open on top of a rosewood credenza, and one door in that credenza remained slightly ajar. Lexi finished opening the door to find a fitted file drawer which slid easily toward her, revealing one, only one, file.

The heavy cardboard folder was organized and compartmented, with pockets and clamps full of papers. And her name. Neatly lettered on a printed label.

With shaking hands Lexi lifted it from the drawer. Working strictly on instinct, she closed the drawer and the door that hid it, checked the hallway and hurried back to her room.

Her sitting room seemed too open, too exposed for the secrecy her theft seemed to demand, and in spite of the fire, it was cold, with sleet once again beating at the windows. Lexi bypassed it and went into her dressing room, where she closed the door on the rest of the house and sank down at her dressing table.

Now that she had the file, did she have the nerve to read it?

No. Of course she didn't. But read it she would.

She hurried past Mel's notes—there would be time for those later—and the nursing notations, which she knew she would have to decipher later for her own peace of mind, to the depth of the file and the beginning history.

According to the record she read, Lexi had presented herself at the clinic in late March and filled out admission papers. She then returned a week later, accompanied by a nurse and had been admitted. She had not been a model patient, often requiring sedation, until the date of her one visitor, the nurse who had accompanied her. Then she had fallen into a deep depression.

The word *depression* had been underlined. A note scribbled in what she recognized as Melissa's handwriting questioned, *Then why?* followed by what she assumed to be the specific name of a drug.

Yes, Lexi thought. Why?

Because even though the newscast last night had said Mel was reported to be the referring physician, Lexi saw no referral report, unless...

A folded report stuck into a pocket overflowing with lab slips caught Lexi's eye. She pulled the report from the folder and smoothed it open. The letterhead bore the name of the clinic she had seen on all the reports, but the name typed for the scrawled signature was Melissa's. Was the signature Melissa's? Lexi simply could not tell.

If there was a reason why she had been admitted to the hospital, she had not yet found it. If there was a reason stated, it would be here, in this report. Quickly Lexi read the few brief pages. It was there, buried at the bottom of page three. And when Lexi found it, she moaned aloud and threw the report from her.

And died a little as she huddled in the womb of her dressing room and remembered, not all, but enough to tease and torture her.

The room beyond her bath. Richard had told her it was not safe. She supposed he was right. How on earth could a nursery be safe for a woman who had killed her unborn child?

And as suddenly as she remembered what the room was, she remembered where she had put the extra key, safely hidden because she used to forget and lock herself out of the room.

Walking very carefully, to keep herself from breaking, Lexi found the key and opened the door. A window was open on the lakeside wall. She crossed the room and closed it, shutting out the draft. She hadn't done much in here, only begun stripping old wallpaper from the walls. She'd thought about refinishing the crib, but had been afraid to do that, afraid the fumes would hurt her unborn baby. The baby she hadn't told Richard about, wouldn't tell him about until a doctor confirmed what she already knew to be true—even though it meant letting him go off to South America with Melissa and hiding from him how ill the brand-new pregnancy had made her.

Two other doors left the room, one to a hallway outside; another to a small suite for a nurse. Lexi shook her head as fuzzy images crowded around her. She'd spent time in that room. Lots of time. And sick. So very sick. But before that, someone else had used the room. Someone—

*It won't work.*

*Yes, it will. He's dead. All we have to do is fire the staff. They know her—*

*And get rid of her.*

*Well, yes. Of course. But that won't be a problem.*

There was a telephone in the far room—with its cord severed to keep her from calling for help in those moments of clarity before someone—someone still hidden from her—urged her to drink. And a hallway outside that room. Dark, narrow, with its unsuspected bank of steps, where she had fled, trying unsuccessfully to escape.

With a moan Lexi dropped to her knees beside the crib. She didn't want to remember this; she didn't want to know this; she couldn't bear this pain.

Richard had been right earlier. The library would not have been a good place to wait. That was where Lexi found all of them, gathered for a meeting that had not included her, until now. Richard and Melissa sat together on the leather sofa. Greg, again in his wheelchair, showed the ravages of the previous night. Helene, imperious, antagonistic even, sat in a wing chair near the fireplace. Eva and Jack Handly. Even a couple of the ominous workmen stood near the door.

All of them looked up at her when she entered the room. "You might as well come in, Lexi. This concerns you, too," Richard said.

He started to rise, but sank back down on the sofa when she threw her medical file with the referral report clipped to the front cover on the table in front of him.

Richard looked from the report to her and blanched.

"Is that what you thought I did, Richard? Killed our child?"

Lexi knew at one level that she wasn't acting rationally, but then, why should she? She was crazy, wasn't she? That was what this file proved. And besides, the pain was too great to do anything rationally.

"Don't you know I would never have done that? He was all I had left of you. You were dead and he was all I had left."

Mel reached for Richard's hand and leaned toward him, and another picture fought its way into Lexi's consciousness. The woman—the shadow woman handing her a picture. *You think he's coming for you? No. Not ever. Why should he?*

Richard and Mel, together on the rattan love seat in the conservatory.

"But you weren't dead, were you? You just didn't want me anymore. Is that why you threw me away?"

Richard stretched his hand toward her. She looked at his hand, tempted beyond all that was swirling uncontrolled through her mind and memory to reach for it. But Helene stood, and in sudden, devastating fear, Lexi backed toward the door. "Stay away from me," she said in a panic-drenched voice, not knowing where the words came from. "I won't let you hurt me. Not again."

Then, whirling, operating only on adrenaline, she ran from the room. She heard the noises behind her, but she had been lost in this house too often not to have learned her way through some of its labyrinthine hallways. Not to have known—how?—where to find a door with an alarm panel she could deactivate so that she could escape undetected from this prison.

She found herself by the kennels before the burst of fear left her. Outside. Dressed only in a sweater and slacks. But she couldn't return to the house. Something horrible had happened there; something horrible waited to happen again. She had to run. Across the overgrown garden toward the safety of the woods. Even though the kennels were empty. Even though as she ran she saw two sleek black forms racing toward her.

Richard sprang up from the sofa, but Mel grabbed his hand. "Let her go. She's safe in the house. We have to see this through."

Was she right? Who knew any more?

But he did know that he had heard terror in his wife's voice when she spoke to Helene. He walked to where Helene stood. She had given him birth, but she had betrayed him, time after time. Each time he had made some excuse or told himself it really didn't matter. But this time there could be no excuse.

"The truth Helene. I will have it. All of it. Now."

The dogs caught Lexi only minutes after she entered the woods. Stumbling, crying, her side aching, Lexi tripped on a vine and went sprawling into the underbrush. She heard them approach and scrambled back against the trunk of a tree, unable to rise, but swearing to herself that she would fight them off.

They approached her, and one, the smaller of the two, whined. Then they stretched out beside her, alert to her every move. Lexi's breath shuddered out of her and she began praying. But she knew there was no escape, because if she were to survive these dogs she must be very sure not to move.

A distant noise woke her. Lexi held her breath, waiting for the answering sound of gunfire that should have followed the sound of the crash, but didn't. And then she remembered that the woods around her were that, woods, and not the jungle where such noises had become commonplace.

She lay propped against the harsh bark of one of Richard's unfamiliar trees, protected by its dense branches and scratchy needly leaves from the ice that spat from a gray sky.

She should have been cold; she was always cold since Richard had brought her to this strange place. But she wasn't. Two sleek black forms lay beside her in the shadow, one on each side of her. She lifted her hand and touched the nearest. Kia. Of course. She was by far the more loving of the two, although Thor, her mate, had been known to beg an extra ear scratch or two when Jack wasn't watching. But only from Lexi. Kia whined and licked Lexi's hand.

"Hello, babies," she said to them. "What are we doing out here in the rain?"

Thor raised his head and crawled closer to her, but neither dog seemed inclined to get up, so Lexi lay there until distant shouts reminded her of the muffled noise that had awakened her, and slowly, image by image, she remembered what had sent her running into the woods, and then quickly, too quickly, images of all that had been blocked from her memory flooded in on her.

"Oh, my dear lord," she whispered and covered her mouth with her hands to keep words and moans from pouring from her. Her fingers touched the dried tracks of tears and she didn't doubt that she'd cried many that day, and would cry more.

She'd run to save her life.

And she'd left Richard there with someone who truly wanted him dead.

Did he know? Did he even suspect the depths of Helene's sickness? And after what she had heard Helene and Greg say, could she be sure that Greg wasn't as much of a threat to Richard as his mother was?

The shadow woman, after all, was trapped in Helene's web, also. Richard's cousin. A cousin he didn't know existed. A cousin who shared his grandfather, but whose mother's existence had been doubted and denied. Did Greg know of her?

Lexi wanted to curl up in the shelter of this tree and grieve for all her losses; she wanted to cry out against the unfairness of life that would allow such evil to exist; she wanted to hide away safely in Richard's arms and never again think of what happened.

But wasn't that same mental denial what had helped keep her in ignorance these past months?

And she could never again hide away safely in Richard's arms if she left him in danger as great as any she had faced.

She swallowed back a lump of fear that gripped her and threatened not to let go. She didn't know what she would do when she got there, but she knew that for Richard's sake she had to return to that monstrosity of a house.

Wherever it was.

Because she had no idea where that might be.

She scrambled to her feet, and Kia and Thor rose to stand beside her. She might not know, but she couldn't remain lost for long. She put one hand on each sleek black head. "Take me home, babies," she said around the fear clogging her throat. "Take me to Richard."

She entered through the same door she had used to flee, and punched in the code to silence the alarm. The dogs hesitated, but she called them into the house with her, and silently, flanked by them, she walked through dark basement halls and narrow stairs until she reached the main hall. One of Richard's workmen met her there. After a quick, surprised glance, he nodded his head and fell in behind her. Friend? Or another enemy? Lexi didn't know and wouldn't stop to ask. She met Jack Handly as she passed the dining room. He smiled at her, a little shocked, and fell in step beside the workman.

Richard was still in the library. Helene had left, but Greg and Melissa were still there, too—Greg standing, leaning over Richard, with his wheelchair overturned as though he had pushed out of it hurriedly, and Mel was handing Richard a cup of something—

"Don't drink it," Lexi said.

Richard looked up, to where she stood in the doorway, with a hand on the head of each dog.

"Move away from him," Lexi ordered the two hovering over him.

Richard closed his eyes and then opened them as he whispered her name. "You're safe."

She nodded. "Yes."

He glanced at the dogs beside her and then met her steady gaze. "I don't think even you can command them to attack me, but I wouldn't blame you for trying. Not knowing what you think I did."

How could she have ever doubted this man—even for a moment?

"I don't think that anymore, Richard. I know what happened."

He blanched but didn't look away from her. "You remember?"

"More than I'd ever want to. But I don't know what part Melissa and Greg played in it, so, please," she said to them again, "move away from him."

She heard the crackle of a radio of some sort in the hall behind her and turned slightly. "My men are calling off the search for you, Lexi," Richard said.

The file still lay on the table. Now two photographs had joined it. She recognized both of them. Their wedding picture. And the picture of Richard and Mel that had been brought to her in the hospital, a picture that had finally broken her spirit and her will to fight. But how had Richard gotten it?

The workman, bodyguard, she now realized, stepped around her and righted Greg's chair. Without a word, he then left the room. Jack coughed slightly. "Why don't I take the dogs, Mrs. Jordan. You really don't need them, you know. There's no danger in this room."

She looked toward Richard. He nodded, and she raised her hands from the dogs' heads. Well trained, obedient, they answered Jack's quiet command and followed him from the room.

Lexi felt her strength leaving her as fast as the tension faded. Now Richard did rise from the couch and cross to her and wrap his arm around her. "I was so worried for you," he said. "I hated each minute that kept me from looking for you."

"Even though I accused you of—of being a part of all that had happened?"

"Wasn't I a part of it?" he asked hoarsely. "Didn't I fall in with her plans by believing her lies?"

Helene. Once again Lexi realized the woman was not in the room. "Where is she?"

Greg seated himself heavily in his chair. "Our dear mother, by now, is in the hospital. After Richard confronted her and she realized she had been found out, she tried to run away and only succeeded in ramming her car into the gatepost. Richard's men freed her from her airbag and got her out relatively unharmed. So I'm pretty sure she'll only spend one night there before she has to worry about bail bonds and attorneys' fees and whether she or my newly discovered cousin will get to turn state's evidence for a reduced sentence."

He laughed but the sound carried the threat of tears.

"I'm sorry, Alexandra. What else can I say? I'm sorry that I didn't know, that I helped make your life a misery, that I *just didn't know*.

"I didn't know she even had a sister, let alone a niece. I didn't know my own mother was capable of such deception and greed.

"And for what...? A house. A damned house."

Melissa had stood quietly. Now she walked to her husband and placed her hands on his shoulders. "I need some of this, too. You were right, Alexandra. I couldn't be objective. I do love Richard, but not as you suspected. I love him because he brought my husband back to me. And I truly thought you had done all you were accused of. Until the evidence began pouring in."

Melissa lifted her head defiantly. "But I'll deal with that later. Right now we're going to the hospital, not because either Greg or I really want to, but because both of us will hate ourselves later if we don't."

They left, and only Lexi and Richard remained in the room that still seemed overfull with accusations and doubts. And love. Lexi reminded herself of that. He loved her. He always had, even when he thought she had betrayed him.

And she loved him, even if he never believed her.

"I can give you one thing you may not know," he said. "One thing that may make some of this a little more bearable."

"Can anything do that, Richard?" She lifted her hands to his face and traced the deep lines that now marked it, and the abrasion that still gave witness to the pain he had suffered. "For me *or* for you?"

"Maybe," he said. "Maybe."

He caught her hands and held them close against his face. "You didn't kill our child," he said, and tightened his hold on her when she flinched and tried to move away. "No one did. You weren't pregnant. Dr. Wilson confirmed that, the night he came to dinner. You had consulted him, you thought you were, but you never returned for your test results. You were ill, Lexi, truly ill, with a bug you must have picked up after we arrived but had no immunity to fight."

The sob tore from her. Now Richard did release her, but only long enough to move his arms around her and hold her while she cried for all the loss and terror and pain of the past months. For him. For her. And for the child that never was. At some point he moved with her to the sofa, but still he held her, until Lexi felt that she would never be able to summon another tear. She hiccuped finally, an inelegant sound, and raised her hands to cup his cheeks, only to find traces of moisture on his harsh, proud face.

"Is there a hotel anywhere within reasonable driving distance?" she asked.

She knew her question had surprised him; he'd so obviously been expecting something else—accusations perhaps? or a litany of blame? But he wouldn't hear that tonight. Not from her.

"There's a state lodge not far from here."

"Can we go there?" she asked. "Just for tonight. And then tomorrow, will you please take me away from this house? We don't need to be here, either of us, ever again. It will make a wonderful museum or art gallery or headquarters for some corporation, but it will never be a home, Richard. Not for us. Not for anyone."

"You're staying with me, then?"

She shook her head and tightened her clasp on his face. "I love you, Richard. One day you'll have to believe me."

"Yes. I guess I will." He smiled at her. "I guess I do. If ever I were tempted to doubt you again, all I have to do is remember you standing in the doorway with your dogs, facing all your nightmares as you returned to rescue me."

Lexi shuddered and slid her arms around him, holding him safe against her. "Let's give up the rescue business," she said. "Both of us."

He nodded. "That sounds like a good idea to me."

"And let's find that lodge," she said.

He was close and warm, and the tension that tightened his body against hers was entirely different from the tension she had felt in him earlier. "And do what?" he asked.

No, she wasn't a coward. Not where this man was concerned. Not where showing him how much he meant to her was the risk she must take.

"And then I thought I'd do something I seem to be getting pretty good at," she told him.

"Oh."

She flashed him a smile full of promise. "I think I'll seduce you."

Richard laughed, and she felt the sound blessing and healing both of them.

"Not seduction," he told her. "I believe the definition of that means one partner is not particularly willing. And, Lexi, that's something I'm never going to be guilty of again."

Now she laughed.

Richard picked her up in his arms and spun her around. For a moment the room seemed to hold them in a strange, slowed moment of time.

Richard set her on her feet and looked around the lavishly appointed library. "Let's get out of here, Mrs. Jordan," he said. "Let's go begin the rest of our life."

* * * * *

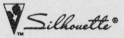

If you enjoyed what you just read,
then we've got an offer you can't resist!

# Take 2 bestselling love stories FREE!

# Plus get a FREE surprise gift!

"Fascinating—you'll want to take
this home!"
—Marie Ferrarella

"Each page is filled with a brand-new
surprise."
—Suzanne Brockmann

"Makes reading a new and joyous
experience all over again."
—Tara Taylor Quinn

See what all your favorite authors
are talking about.

*Coming October 1999 to a retail store near you.*